D0919721

TIME'S FOOL

LIBRARY OF

TIME'S FOOL

GRANT CARRINGTON

DOUBLEDAY & COMPANY, INC.
GARDEN CITY, NEW YORK
1981

All of the characters in this book
are fictitious, and any resemblance
to actual persons, living or dead,
is purely coincidental.

First Edition

ISBN: 0-385-15288-4
Library of Congress Catalog Card Number 79–8558
Copyright © 1981 by Grant Carrington
All Rights Reserved
Printed in the United States of America

This one is for my mother.

But thought's the slave of life, and life, time's fool;
And time, that takes survey of all the world,
Must have a stop.

King Henry IV, Part I
William Shakespeare
Act V, Scene 4

TIME'S FOOL

CHAPTER 1

Waves of conversation crested on Garcia's ears, like the somnolent disharmonies of Vlatko's "Modular" Symphony, as the autarist moved through the party. He stopped to flirt briefly with a young synthesist who wore one of Amiloun's programmable gowns. This one writhed about the young synthesist's body slowly, changing colors and iridescing, revealing and concealing, its movements programmed to display its host's finest features to their best advantage.

Justin Mead gestured to Garcia from the other side of the room and Garcia moved over to his side. Justin's knotted and gnarled hand carried the flute that he played so beautifully. "How about a duet?"

"Certainly." Garcia picked up the guitar nearby. For a few moments the two friends weaved melodies and harmonies, Garcia dropping into straight rhythm while Justin's flute swooped and soared, spreading crystalline notes through the party, then Justin played low throaty soft warbles while Garcia plucked arpeggios, triplets, and two- and three-note chords from his instrument.

When they were done, the people clustered around them applauded. Justin looked at Garcia. "Your choice," he said.

Garcia held up his hand. "Not right now. Maybe later."

Justin's creased face became even more lined with concern. "Is something wrong, Garcia? You don't usually settle for just one song."

"No, nothing's wrong, Justin."

"You're sure?"

"I'm sure."

But as he moved away from his friend, Garcia wasn't so certain. He had hoped that playing music with Justin would quell the undercurrent of dissatisfaction that refused to identify itself but, instead, it had seemed to intensify the feeling. There had been no satisfaction at music well-played, once again sharing the moment with Justin. It seemed he had done it too many times before.

He stood at his false fireplace, staring at the simulated fire, the faint scent of cedar drifting past his nostrils. The glass of dark cognac in his hand was forgotten, and the party's hum, the polychords of disconnected conversations, went past him unheard.

"Don't look so sad, Garcia." A pretty girl ran her hand up his real arm. Garcia smiled briefly at her and turned away. Garcia did not often turn away from a pretty girl.

Shrill laughter burst over the conversational hum, like a discordant trumpet solo.

Garcia's agent, Renard, was talking to a moderately attractive girl, one of the few at the party whom Garcia did not already know. Her sharp-featured face had an alert, lively expression that he found quite attractive, although a number of the women present were considerably more physically attractive than she.

"Have you met Shaara yet?" Renard asked.

"No, I don't think so. She must have slipped in when I wasn't looking."

She smiled at him warmly. "I'm pleased to meet you." Her handshake was firm and unfeminine.

"Shaara," Garcia repeated.

"That's right."

"She wanted to meet you, Garcia, so I brought her along. She's Muenstretiger's daughter."

"Muenstretiger." The name was familiar, but Garcia couldn't place it.

"He's the chairman of Merck & Muenstretiger. Pharmaceuticals?"

"Oh. Yes." It was the largest of the pharmaceutical firms.

"She's made a bit of a reputation on her own, as a plastic artist. She's having an exhibition of her mobile art down at Dr. Hawk's."

Garcia turned to Shaara. "This palace must appear rather poor to you."

"I'm afraid I *do* find it a bit tasteless." Shaara's smile softened the impact of her words. "I really had expected better of you."

They were standing in the doorway to Garcia's bedroom. A varibed, now dialed to soft, dominated one corner of the room. Ancient prints, some of them erotic, adorned the earthy red-brown walls. The floor was covered with a shaggy Oriental carpet heavily laced with muted black and orange designs.

"You seem to be obsessed with royal themes." She looked around into the main room, where Garcia's friends were busy chatting, drinking, playing instruments, and singing. That room was sunk about two feet below the level of his bedroom, so that Garcia's entrances were always down to it, majestic and royal. He had often enjoyed "holding court" in that room, sitting in the conspicuously spartan chair in front of the fireplace, listening to the conversation and only occasionally deigning to speak a few words or to play a short melody on his guitar. He would sit there regally, smiling on his favorites, tossing tidbits into the unreal fire. It was all a game, really; he consciously realized it for the first time as he looked over Shaara's shoulder.

The whole thing now seemed devoid of interest and savor. It was a thing of childhood, something to be put aside. But what was there to take its place?

"What are you scowling about? I didn't mean to offend you."

Broken rudely out of his reverie, Garcia stuttered for a moment. "Oh, you didn't offend me. I was just thinking." He gestured at the main room. "Perhaps you're right. I *do* seem to have an obsession with royalty. Medieval royalty at that."

All the main room's pretensions now hung over him. He had once pictured it as a medieval Spanish castle, with banners and standards hanging from the walls, a few wolfhounds wandering among the guests, flagons of wine, stone walls and roaring fires, with balladeers and full-skirted women roaming through the halls.

Instead he had a meager unreal fire, a carefully random selection of chairs and seats, plush rugs, and a retinue of sycophants. He himself was the balladeer, the minstrel, whose artificial fingers played melodies with more precision and feeling than anyone else ever had before.

Or was he merely the fool?

"It *does* kind of suit you."

"How's that?"

"I have this picture of you, an overblown romantic fantasy, I'm afraid, where you're standing on a bluff overlooking the ocean, wearing a cape that's blowing in the wind."

Garcia frowned. It was too close to his own fantasies for comfort.

"You don't like that."

"You're right. It *is* a bit overblown."

She touched his arm. "Do you . . . do you mind talking about this?"

Garcia smiled. She had been touching his real arm. "There's not much to say about that one."

"There's not? I thought . . ." She stopped, blushing, as she realized her mistake. "I . . . I . . . but the other one looks so real."

Garcia reached up to his right shoulder and detached the arm. His sleeve hung empty as he handed the arm to the girl. She took it gingerly. "But it's warm!"

"They can do wonders with electronics and plastic." Garcia was uncomfortable. The arms were all part of him; he felt naked without one, no matter how much clothing he might be wearing.

She handed it back to him and he quickly locked it back into place.

"I knew my father was doing wonderful things in the

prosthetics line. I've used some of his techniques myself in some of my sculptures. But I hadn't realized he'd gone this far."

"Well, they're quite expensive, believe me. At least, for a musician. And I need several of them."

"How many do you have?"

"Five."

"What do you need that many for?"

"I have two performance arms. They look just like my social arms, but they're more sensitive and complicated. And, of course, they're programmed to play the autar."

"Programmed?"

"Well, not exactly. But there are things I can do with them that I can't do with my social arms. The fingers are more flexible and I have a finer sense of touch and more delicacy. But I wouldn't dare shake hands with them and I certainly wouldn't do anything with them that required any strength."

"You play quite well with that arm." She indicated the one he was wearing.

"Yes. It's an all-purpose arm, what's called a social arm. It's capable of doing just about anything that can be done with a real arm. So I can play guitar quite competently with it. Or autar."

"That accounts for three of your arms. What about the other two?"

"I have another social arm, a spare, and the other one is for doing delicate manual labor. Instead of fingers, it has tools, test probes, and other appendages. It even has a kind of an eye."

"An eye? What on Earth for?"

"It's very handy for working inside my autar. That's what the arm is for, working on my instruments."

"I'd think you would have someone else do that for you. You certainly can afford it."

"Yes, I can. But working on my own instruments helps me understand them better, learning their limitations and how to work with them instead of against them. It's another facet of being a performer, one that many entertainers ignore."

"I see . . . I think."

"Don't worry about it." He held his hand out. She took it and they descended to the main room. The staged effect of their return to the party made Garcia very uncomfortable.

CHAPTER 2

At last Garcia was alone; everyone had gone, and he was finally able to stand still and think. But his thoughts wouldn't hold still long enough for him to grab onto them.

He walked to the doorway and leaned his weight against it, both hands against the sills. The main room was empty; there was no one in it to whom he could play lord. It was just as well: he was wearing only a pair of tight-fitting bright red trunks now, and they looked ludicrous on his stocky body, emphasizing his nascent obesity. His stomach hung slightly over the trunks in rolls of fat that refused to go away. He thought of Justin's slender, reedlike body with rueful envy.

His hair was tousled and unkempt, sticking out in all directions. He fancied that he looked like a Spanish don surveying his domain, and he was fully aware of it and did nothing to change his mien. He was also aware that he was his own best audience, and that he enjoyed these little games, like a little child playing at being lost adrift on the sea, making a raft out of a few chairs and a seat.

Ordinarily, he could draw on his emotions for the power and strength that poured out of him when he was in the spotlight, even on his unhappiness and uneasiness, but now there was a restlessness that underlined his unhappiness in a manner that he couldn't enjoy.

He picked up a glass of wine and stared into it. It was calm and unperturbed but when he started to swirl it, a vortex formed in the middle. Meanwhile, at the edges of the wine, eddies formed and broke up, battling each other, so transient that they were barely formed before they destroyed themselves, while the central vortex remained coherent. It was like his own thoughts and emotions, moving too fast for identification, breaking up and reforming even as he tried to examine them, Heisenberg's principle in action among the electrochemical synapses of his mind.

He sipped the wine. It was warm and flat, as his life had become. Its edge was gone. At first he had enjoyed the attentions of his meteoric rise to fame. No one else approached his mastery of the autar, which some claimed to be one of the most complex and difficult instruments ever invented. Nor had his rise to fame been slowed by an incident that had occurred early in his career, an event that already was beginning to attain mythic status.

It had been only five years since Garcia, already established as a performer, met Stella Blue, a time-dipper who had met the composer Radcliffe while on a research trip and fallen in love with him. She had returned to her own time (and Garcia's), been cashiered from the time-dippers, and was making her living as a guitarist in a tiny club in the *barraque* when Garcia first heard her and fell in love with her and her sad and plaintive music. His entreaties had only resulted in her attempted suicide; in saving her, Garcia had lost his arm. Its replacement was more sensitive and versatile than the original, but it was not that which was primarily responsible for his subsequent meteoric career. Stella Blue had committed suicide while Garcia was recovering, and the whole experience and emotions found their outlet in his music. A new dimension was added to Garcia's performances, which had been clean and faultless before, but colorless, without fire. Now an inner fire burned and consumed his performance.

Was it that same fire that now was reaching into his private life, that refused to let him alone? Or, instead, was the fire dying and its embers winking out, leaving him alone and hollow, like a deaf musician? Garcia stared into the wine and wondered. At last he put it down and walked back to the bedroom. He pulled aside an Oriental tapestry and unlocked the door behind it.

The room thus uncovered lacked the opulence of Garcia's other rooms. It was antiseptic and sound-absorbent. In airtight cabinets on one wall of the room were Garcia's instruments: the ancient autar supposedly invented by Radcliffe himself; the guitar that Stella Blue had been playing when Garcia first met her. Two other modern-day autars were in their cases under the display cabinets. Recording machines lined another wall, with inset directional microphones that could be swiveled to point wherever needed.

In a corner of the cabinet, near Stella Blue's guitar, were pictures of her and Radcliffe, and a tape of Radcliffe's last performance, a clumsy and awkward performance, but one with more power and fire than Garcia had ever been able to summon.

He touched a spot on the one blank wall in the room and part of that wall went transparent, revealing an awesome view of the city. Lights stretched out in front of Garcia and to the sides, more or less orderly, for most of the residents were asleep. But the lights of all-night establishments and factories and power stations still burned, forming blocks of luminescence among the strings of street lights. Bridges were necklaces of light, like spiderwebs hung with morning dew, and the river flowed sluggishly, glowing faintly, underneath them. It was here that Stella Blue had drowned herself; it was here that Garcia had lost his arm to the mouth of a river cleaner while stopping her first attempt.

He unlocked the cabinet and took out her guitar. He had scorned such simple instruments before he met her, but since her death he had mastered it, marveling at the raw emotions it evoked and at the nuances he was able to attain with such a basic instrument. He had been so smug and self-satisfied before he met her, completely oblivious to a whole world of emotions and abilities that were just outside the periphery of his knowledge. It had been a simple world, but he would not go back to it if he could; it seemed a drab and colorless life, atonal and monotone, compared to the kaleidoscopic life he now knew.

He played the guitar for fifteen minutes, beginning with a simple progression of single notes that rapidly wove themselves into a complex cascade of harmonies and counterpoint, then dying back to the simple progression of single notes. It was his farewell to Stella Blue, the only composition he had ever written, which he had never performed publicly, a hymn of thanks to her, and a paean.

He returned to the main room, poured himself a large glass of wine, turned off the lights, and tried to drink himself to sleep. Stars and planets played gently on his ceiling, and soft music played from the wall. But it was still a long time to dawn.

CHAPTER 3

The decayed and ancient face of Bwire, Garcia's most famous tutor, peered at Garcia before finally recognizing him. "What do you want this time?" His cracked and broken voice carried no trace of the once-rich baritone that had often castigated Garcia mercilessly. "Always to me you come when you're in trouble. It is what this time?"

Bwire settled back down in his chair. His apartment was spare compared to the opulence of Garcia's, but it was the sparseness of a once-sharp mind. There was nothing here that didn't belong, that had no purpose; similarly, nothing was missing.

"I can't stay long." Garcia nervously brushed back his dark hair and sat on the edge of one of the other chairs. He could barely hear the hum of the city outside Bwire's windows.

"I know, I know." Bwire waved a peevish hand. "That old bag won't let anyone stay any longer than a goddamn waver of her goddamn instruments."

The "old bag" to whom Bwire referred was the nurse who had admitted Garcia with the admonition, "You can't stay long. He gets excited and then it's all I can do to keep him from having another attack."

"Sometimes," Bwire said, "I wish they'd just let me die and get it over with."

"Oh no." Garcia genuinely desired the old man to live. He would miss him deeply.

"Only yourself you think of." Garcia wondered what Bwire was referring to; his attention wandered more and more as he grew older, until sometimes it was impossible to figure out what he was talking about. But sometimes it was just Bwire's oblique way of referring to things. "It is what this time?"

"I wish I knew." He tried to find the words to explain his uneasiness, but there were none. "At the party last night I . . . well, I couldn't enjoy myself."

"I never cared for parties myself." The old man's voice was sharp and critical, as if to say that parties were pointless and a waste of valuable time.

"But that's the point!" The words burst from Garcia. "I've always enjoyed parties, but this time . . ."

"You didn't get your usual attention?" A smile played at the edges of Bwire's mouth.

"No, it wasn't that. I just didn't enjoy the attention as much. I felt like . . . like the third movement of Radcliffe's last sonata."

Bwire raised an eyebrow. The smile was gone from his face. "The one he wrote before committing suicide."

The thought had not occurred to Garcia. "Yes, but I'm not . . ."

"I know, I know." Bwire shifted in his chair, trying to find a nonexistent comfortable spot. "Do you remember what Radcliffe wrote then?" Garcia shook his head. " 'I have tried to find something in music, but it wasn't there. Perhaps it never had been. Perhaps it was just a worm. Without the worm, I would never have done what little I have, like a tiny rosebush in a vast garden. Without the worm, there would have been no roses.'"

"I'm not sure I . . ."

"So you didn't enjoy your adulation last night?"

"No. There was a woman there . . ."

Bwire smiled again. "Isn't there *always* a woman there?"

"She . . . she was very critical of my apartment, and she was right, she got me to thinking. . . ."

"So? To thinking of what?"

"I'm not sure. But I feel as if I've lost touch with my music, that it's become just a means to more adulation, to silly childish belongings, and not an end in itself."

And once it had been. Once Garcia had lived for his music. It had never palled on him, but slowly, insidiously, without his even being aware of its loss, it had been drained away from him.

Bwire leaned back in his chair and closed his eyes. "You are the finest autarist who has ever lived, Garcia." He opened his eyes, fastening them on his former pupil. "I do not say that lightly. But you have so much to learn as a human being."

"But there's so much left to learn as . . ."

". . . as a musician?" The old master leaned forward in his chair. "Who is there for you to learn from? Who is there who can do anything on the autar that you can't?"

"No one," Garcia said softly. "No one that I know of."

"Is there anyone who plays faster than you, who has a surer touch, who can play any kind of music better than you?" Garcia shook his head. "Where do you go now, Garcia? What do you do now?"

"I don't know." Garcia's voice was a whisper.

"Is there anyone but you who can play that piece that Carter wrote for you?"

"I don't think so."

The old man put his gnarled hands on the arms of his chair and pushed himself up. He walked painfully over to the simple window that looked out over the sunlit city. Outside that window, the impersonal and antiseptic face of the city stared uncaring at the two musicians. Bwire stared defiantly back at it for a long moment before turning back to Garcia.

"Hard," he said. "It *is* hard." He walked over and placed his hand on Garcia's shoulder. "In many ways, you are my own son, and you suffer, I suffer. Your arm, I grieved and hurt too when you lost it."

"I know," Garcia said softly.

"But now it is time for you to grow again, and there is no help that I can give. You need to reach outside yourself, Garcia; you need to be more than a performer."

The words meant little to Garcia; they touched no sensitive spot inside him. When he added them to the inchoate roil of his emotions, they clarified nothing.

"What do you suggest?" he asked at last.

"A student perhaps."

"I'm no teacher."

"You should be, perhaps."

"I couldn't teach anyone. I don't have enough patience."

"I'll contact the conservatory. I'll have them send their best student." Garcia started to protest, but the old man held up his hand. "No. Listen, Garcia. Only to try, that's all I ask of you. To reach beyond yourself, to help someone else." He paused. "Was I so wrong before?" he asked softly.

"No." Garcia remembered how Bwire had helped him find Stella Blue when he was looking frantically for her. But he was uncertain: had he not found her, she might still be alive and he would still have his arm. On the other hand, his music would perhaps still be clinically pure and emotionally dead: sterile. It seemed that nothing ever came for free, that nothing of value was ever bought without pain.

CHAPTER 4

Garcia's first student, a young man named Jorme, was tall and gangling, with large, clumsy, awkward hands. He didn't seem to know what to do with them and they were in constant motion, pointless movements that had neither beginning nor end. His long oval face was pocked with pimples and had an unattractive marbled appearance. This was the young man who Bwire had assured Garcia was the most advanced student at the conservatory.

Jorme was carrying one of the most expensive mass-production autars, a GBM 60K, its finish already showing the wear of much use and playing.

"Sit down." Garcia felt nearly as awkward as Jorme appeared. "Would you care for some wine?"

"Uh, sure." Jorme sat stiffly on the edge of the least comfortable chair in the room, the one in which Garcia usually sat himself.

"Relax." Garcia poured two glasses of wine. "I'm not sure I'll be able to help you very much. You're the first student I've ever had."

"You are? I mean, I am?" Jorme's hands wandered aimlessly over the autar case. "That's . . . that's quite an honor. I mean, being *your* first student."

"It might be something of a disaster." Garcia handed the wine to Jorme. "I don't quite know how to begin."

Jorme said nothing, waiting until Garcia started to sip his
wine before he did so himself, copying Garcia. "Well,
maybe you'd just better play something for me, so I'll
know what you can do."

Jorme began with a simple exercise, which he executed
flawlessly, despite his obvious nervousness. "I hope you can
do something more complex than that," Garcia said sarcas-
tically, surprised to hear in the tone of his voice the same
mannerisms that Bwire had used with him.

"I just thought I'd . . . I'd start with something easy
and work my way up."

"Keep going." Garcia tried to keep Bwire's wry sarcasm
out of his voice, but the effort was unsuccessful.

Jorme went through increasingly more difficult pieces,
making occasional nervous mistakes that happened less frequently as he became more absorbed in the music. Technique was not Jorme's strong point: as he began to perform
concert pieces, Garcia could see that his forte was the fire
and drive that Garcia's own early performances had lacked.
But, though Jorme always played the correct notes, his
style lacked the crispness and clarity of Garcia's.

"Here! Wait a minute." Garcia interrupted Jorme's playing. The youngster looked up, his face looking as though
he expected to be chastised, a puppy about to be whipped.
"Listen to this." Garcia played the last four bars that
Jorme had played. "Do you see the difference?"

"I . . . I'm not sure."

"Play it again." Jorme played a bar and a half, and Garcia stopped him. "Your phrasing is sloppy on that triplet.
Listen." Garcia played it again. "Do you see?"

"I think so." Jorme was hesitant.

For the next half hour they continued in that vein, Garcia trying to correct Jorme's lack of clarity. It was very frustrating: it was so clear and obvious what was wrong, but he had trouble finding the words to explain it. Frequently Jorme claimed he couldn't see any difference and, when he did, he was unable to correct himself. He even argued once with Garcia that his own version was better. Only one time was he able to duplicate Garcia's performance.

When Jorme at last was gone, Garcia felt drained. It was far more exhausting than a concert! It forced him to question his own biases and the techniques that had become second nature to him. Explaining to someone else what he did was far more difficult than actually doing it.

But there was a feeling of exultation to the experience as well, not as profound as that he had once known as a performer, but a strong echo of that feeling, and he welcomed it. Perhaps there *was* more, after all. Still, he didn't feel that teaching would ever be as fulfilling and important to him as actually making the music himself.

Restless and excited, he took an electrocab down to his agent's office to talk about his upcoming concert tour. When he mentioned that he had taken on a student, Renard frowned. "I don't like it," he said. "This is going to interfere with your concentration. It's going to be a drain on your energies."

Garcia watched Renard's secretary, who was querying the computer terminal. "I don't think so," he said. "It might even help me."

"How could it?"

"It's making me think more about what I'm doing, making me more aware of what's going on when I play the autar."

"And you think that's good?"

"Isn't it?"

"You ever heard about the centipede who started to think about which leg went first and fell flat on its face?"

Garcia stifled the urge to argue. "That could happen, I guess. But if it does, I'll just have to quit teaching, that's all. Don't worry about it."

"Yeah, yeah. By the time you realize what's happening, it'll already be too late. You'll be thinking too much."

"Don't worry about it." Garcia punched Renard lightly and playfully on the shoulder. "You've already made your bundle off me. And, hell, I'll still know what I'm doing. It won't work that way, believe me, Renard."

"Sure, sure."

"By the way, what happened to that girl you brought to my party the other night?"

"Shaara?"

"Yeah. What do you know about her?"

"Interested?"

"A little."

"Forget it. She's not your type."

"Afraid I'll steal her from you?"

Renard smiled. "Not at all. She's too rich for my blood. Totally out of my class. There's nothing between us and there never will be."

"Then what were you doing with her?"

"She wanted to meet you. And it doesn't hurt to indulge the rich. You're a hot item, you know."

"So you keep telling me."

Renard's secretary turned to the two men. "Everything's ready now, sir."

"Okay. Thanks, Lyana. Let's take a look at what I've lined up for your next concert series." Renard pressed the button on the display unit on his desk. "Incidentally, Shaara would like you to come to a party her father's giving next week."

"What?" Garcia couldn't stifle the grin that arose at his agent's nonsequiturs and self-contradictions.

"You heard me," Renard said wryly. "She'll send a chauffeur for you. Enjoy it. Now . . . your tour starts two weeks from tomorrow right here in town. We've got just enough time to advertise what you're going to perform. Have you decided yet?"

CHAPTER 5

Mars Ruby ran her nails lightly over the coarse dark hair of Garcia's chest. "You're putting on weight," she said.

"I know. I can't seem to help it."

"You're going to get fat." Garcia grimaced. "What's this?"

"What's what?"

"Oh, isn't that cute?" She smiled coquettishly at him.

"What is it?" he asked in irritation. He sat up, trying to see what she was looking at.

"See it? Right there." She pulled a small tuft of hair straight out. "It's a white hair. You're growing old too, Garcia."

"Is that all?" Garcia lay back again, disgruntled.

"Old and fat. Soon you'll be old and fat. What will you do then?"

"Will you quit making such a big thing out of it?"

"My, aren't you the irritable one today. What's bothering you?"

"Nothing's bothering me. Nothing but you."

"Garcia?" Her voice took a placating, querulous tone. "It isn't going to help if you keep it inside you. What's wrong?" She ran her hand gently through his curly black hair. He wondered if she was seeing gray strands there as well.

"I'm not sure."

"Are you in love?"

"Don't be silly. Of course not."

"What about that girl at your party? What was her name? Shaara?"

"Give me credit for *some* brains."

"Love has nothing to do with brains. Look at Justin and *his* wife."

"He loves her."

"Yes, of course he does. But he could do so much better."

"She's a damn good musician."

"And I'm a damn good lover. Do you love me?"

"Of course." Garcia pulled her close to him but, after a short moment of acquiescence, she pulled away.

"But you're not in love with me."

"What's the difference?"

"There's a big difference." She shook her head and her long red hair tossed around on her back. "Do you want to marry me?"

Garcia thought for a moment, trying to find a way to tell the truth without hurting Ruby's feelings.

"Forget it. It's obvious you don't. Don't worry about it. I like you a lot, Garcia, but I wouldn't want to spend the rest of my life with you."

"Oh." Garcia was slightly disturbed by her statement. He moved toward the edge of the bed.

"Now *I've* hurt *you*."

"No, you haven't. Really."

She sighed and moved over to his side, caressing his

back. "You're so mixed up, Garcia. I wish I knew what was wrong. I wish I knew how to help you."

"Bwire thinks being a teacher will help."

"It doesn't?"

Garcia shook his head slowly. "No. I enjoy it more than I thought I would. Jorme's a nice kid, and I think we're going to be friends."

"Good. You need another friend."

He turned to face her. "But it's not enough. There's something . . . I don't know, like something missing. Teaching fills it a little bit, but not enough."

"Performing isn't enough?"

"It doesn't seem to be. Not any more." How could he explain it to her? He had come to the end of the road of his development as an autarist, and there were no challenges left, no new roads to conquer.

He dimmed the already-faint light in the room.

"Maybe you ought to try something else. Like another instrument." Garcia made a gruff disparaging sound in his throat. "You ought to see Gang's Fool."

"Another of your popular groups?"

"Cotton Jennie's body is so in tune with her computer, it's just incredibly smooth, and Amis plays rhythms on his percusser that are almost as complex as *grilly*."

"But there's no feedback to those systems."

"Sure there is. They don't use it often, but it's there."

Garcia sighed. "I don't mean electronic feedback."

"What are you talking about, then?"

"The feedback a performer gets from his instrument. The tension of the strings, the way they respond under his fingers. You don't get that kind of feedback from completely computerized music, and so you can't get the nuances, the subtleties. Do you know what I mean?"

Mars Ruby moved under the covers, trying to find a comfortable position. "I don't think you *want* to listen to them. Your mind is closed."

He stared at the stars on his ceiling, moving as imperceptibly and as surely as the ones in the sky, and exactly in tune with them. Was she right, or was it her mind that was closed? He didn't know the answer.

"Let's get some sleep." His hands moved briefly over the bed's controls and the cool spring breeze of a long-forgotten New England evening played gently over their bodies.

CHAPTER 6

"Ready to call it quits?"

"Yeah." Jorme laid his autar down and wiped his forehead with the back of his forearm. "That was rough."

"It sure was." Garcia's voice was sardonic.

"I really don't see why you think it's so important, though. So what if it isn't quite as clean and sharp as it could be? Only half a dozen people'll know the difference."

"*You'll* know." Garcia brushed back a lock of his dark hair.

"So what?"

"Look at it this way, Jorme." Garcia poured some wine. "Sure, no one else knows the difference . . . now. But being *able* to do it, well, that gives you so much more freedom, so many more options when you perform. And, when you record, your recorded performance is going to last a hell of a lot longer if your attack is clean and sharp."

"What are you getting at?"

"Maybe only half a dozen people know the difference now. But ten years from now it'll be half a hundred. And then more, and more. And something else will be on the outside edges of technique, where only half a dozen people can appreciate it. And, who knows? Maybe *you'll* be the guy who comes up with it."

"Yeah." Jorme grinned. "Wouldn't that be something?" He took the glass from Garcia and began drinking, more confidently than before.

"I'm sure you will. You've got the ability."

"You really think so?" Jorme looked at his hands. "Sometimes I wonder. Did you ever wonder whether you'd make it?"

Garcia smiled. "No. I guess I always knew I would. It was just a matter of time. I got pretty impatient sometimes, though."

"I wish I could be that certain. I mean, everybody says I'm good. You're not the first, but it really means quite a lot coming from you, you know?"

"You wouldn't be here if a lot of people didn't think you were damn good. I don't have time to waste on amateurs."

"But I'm scared. I mean, with all the performances I've given at schools and things, you'd think I wouldn't get stage fright. But the thought of really going out on my own and giving my *own* performance, not just one with a lot of other students, it scares me."

"There's nothing to be scared of." It was one more thing about Jorme that Garcia couldn't comprehend: he himself had always been a performer; it was what he lived for. It was the loss of that edge that now distressed him.

"I know, I know." Jorme began pacing the room. "A lot of the other students feel that way. About half of them have already given solo concerts. I'm just about the only one who hasn't who's near the top of things."

"You're not near the top. You're *at* the top."

"You think so? You really think so?"

"Of course. You're the top student at the school. That's

why you're here." It was incomprehensible that Jorme could have come so far without having had a solo concert. They were so completely different from each other, coming at the same thing from completely different angles. And yet . . . Jorme had talent and lots of it. If he only had the confidence to go with it, he would be unbeatable. Garcia sat down in the chair that Jorme had vacated. "And it's time you had a solo concert of your own."

"I don't think I'm quite ready."

"You'll never be quite ready. You're good, damn good, Jorme, and it's time you went out on your own. I'm going to talk to Renard and see if he'll take you on as a client. Do you mind?"

"Well . . . no. But I don't think he likes me."

Garca smiled. "It has nothing to do with you. He just doesn't like the idea of me teaching anybody. He thinks I'll lose my touch if I have to analyze what I'm doing. He forgets that all my technique and craft are based on a very thorough analysis of the autar and what it can do."

"I'm still not sure it's a good idea."

"Wait a minute!" Garcia rose suddenly from the chair, facing Jorme, his eyes twinkling. "I've got an idea. We can perform together. You and me. That way I can keep teaching you. What a promotional stunt. Garcia and his first student. His first protégé. Hey! What do you think?"

"I think it's scary."

"I'm sure Renard will go for it."

Garcia asked the supervisor for a line to his agent, eager to share the idea with Renard. But after he had outlined the entire idea, Reynard said, "I think it's dumb."

"But you'll do it?"

"Do I have any choice?"

Garcia regarded the ceiling in a studied pose of contemplation. "I could go to work at the conservatory as a teacher."

"I'll think about it."

Garcia closed the connection and turned to Jorme, who was frowning. "Don't worry about it. He'll come around."

CHAPTER 7

The cranky, crotchety Bwire whom Garcia was used to, even fond of, was gone, replaced by a more introspective and reminiscing Bwire. He sat in his chair, seeming to have shrunk even in the short time since Garcia had last seen him. "So, you and Jorme will share concerts? A good move. Grow, Garcia, grow. Stagnate, and you die. Inside, a piece of you dies. Enough pieces die, and what are you? A technician, a craftsman, yes, but not human. Not really human."

"Of course," Garcia said politely.

"This is a good thing for you. Like Stella Blue. It will be hard, yes, that I know, but it must be done. Don't ever doubt it, Garcia. Don't ever doubt it." The old man reached out and gripped Garcia's real arm, gripping it tightly, almost painfully, a claw, a talon, ripping into Garcia's flesh. At first Garcia recoiled at the touch from this ancient flesh, but he caught that move before it had barely begun, relaxed, and covered Bwire's hands with his own. And in that simple act he remembered the supple and flexible fingers that had taught him so much of what he knew about the autar; he looked briefly into his own future, seeing his own fingers grow gnarled and knotty. But on one hand they would remain smooth and supple, capable. Or would his nerves decay also, so that he would lose control even of his artificial arm?

"Play for me, Garcia. Play for an old man."

"I didn't bring my autar with me. I'm sorry. I really am." And he was. It had been a long time since he had played for the old master.

But Bwire only smiled. "Really, Garcia, you don't think that I would be without an autar, do you? Even now?" Bwire's voice caught briefly, but when he spoke again, after a very brief pause, there was no edge of emotion to it. "Over there. To your left." As he spoke, he pressed buttons on his chair, and a cabinet that had been opaque grew transparent; its top slowly tilted back to reveal the venerable autar that Bwire had often played for Garcia.

"But . . . I couldn't . . ." Garcia started to say.

"Please," the old man whispered. "It was meant to be played and it will be yours one day."

Garcia picked the instrument up carefully. It had been handmade by Althor Burn, the same craftsman who had made two of his own concert instruments, but this one had been made thirty years earlier, when Althor Burn was just making a reputation for himself. It was simpler, less versatile, but Garcia was used to that, having played the ancient instrument that had reputedly belonged to Radcliffe. Such instruments demanded more from the performer than the more complex modern ones. But this was Bwire's instrument and, as such, it meant even more to Garcia.

He powered the instrument and began playing, softly, delicately, starting with simple computer harmonies, shifting keys fluently, while Bwire sat with his eyes closed, smiling. Garcia played the music of Radcliffe and of Scheiner, of Thomas the Rhymer and of Mooncat. He played his own transcription of one of Stella Blue's songs, the computer playing a sitaresque wailing behind his own raw strumming, simple but powerful. And finally he played some of Bwire's own compositions, impishly sneaking in one of the exercises that Bwire originally had given him.

The old master opened his eyes and grinned. "Very nice, Garcia. You know, five years ago, that was something you wouldn't have done."

Garcia nodded. "It wouldn't even have occurred to me."

"And where will you be when you return, I wonder? What will you be like? I will be very curious to find out. It will be worth living for." He rose very wearily from his chair and walked over to Garcia. The old, once-agile claw gripped Garcia's shoulder. "Come back as soon as possible, Garcia."

"I will." His voice was almost a whisper. "As soon as I can."

CHAPTER 8

Shaara agreed to let Garcia bring Jorme to the party, and the young autarist was at Garcia's apartment long before Muenstretiger's chauffeur arrived. He was dressed in ill-fitting brand-new garments and was just as nervous as he had been when he had arrived for his first lesson, if not more so.

"Do I look all right?" he asked Garcia.

"You look fine." There was no sense in telling Jorme how he really appeared.

"I'm so afraid I'll make a fool of myself. I've never been to a place like this before."

"If it'll make you feel any better, neither have I."

"How can you be so calm?"

Garcia shrugged. "What else is there to do?" How could he possibly explain to Jorme? Even if Garcia had never been to a party at the estate of someone as rich and powerful as Muenstretiger, he had been to enough parties held by some of the more influential people in the city, and they were all the same: a bore.

When the chauffeur at last arrived, Jorme had already gulped down two glasses of wine and his nervousness had abated somewhat. Muenstretiger's own private vehicle purred electrically through the streets until they reached the estate. It was ringed by a high stone wall with barbed wire at the top. The vehicle stopped at a massive gate that finally swung open on ponderous hinges.

They rode along a long graveled driveway through a parklike expanse to a large mansion that was in perfect condition. Stately trees lined the roadway, but a large spacious lawn surrounded the house.

"They're really cautious about intruders, aren't they?" Jorme said.

"Wouldn't you be?"

"I guess it's a holdover from the riots."

A liveried butler, not a robot, greeted them and led them to a large hall, full of people milling about, and announced them even as Shaara and her father were coming toward them. Muenstretiger moved swiftly and surely, like a wolf set loose in a sheepfold. His full head of hair was completely white but the eyebrows were still dark. He took Garcia's hand in a grip that was firm yet not too firm. "I'm pleased to meet you, Garcia. I've enjoyed listening to you play and it's a pleasure to meet you in person." His voice was rich and full, without being overly loud. It was the voice of a man with power and money, a man who was certain of himself, a man who needed no ostentation to feel secure. Garcia had never had to worry about money in his entire life, but he was a pauper compared to this man.

He muttered the usual inane social amenities and introduced Jorme.

"Yes, your student. Well, I've never heard you play, young man, but I'm sure you must be most accomplished. I look forward to hearing you some day."

Jorme stuttered out his thanks.

"Shaara, why don't you take them over to the bar?"

She had been silent during the greetings, but Garcia kept meeting her eyes, seeing a small quiet smile on her face. It was hard to say anything to her while her father was there. In the gaudy company of the party, she seemed drab and unspectacular. Her face was sharp and angular; her nose was crooked; and her hair was cut severely short. Garcia had always been enamored of long hair. Everything about her was wrong and nothing was right. She was short and slim, her figure more boyish than womanly; her breasts were small bumps, not the ripe and pendulant fruits of some of the more generously-endowed women at the party. Her shimmering blouse was closed at the throat, and her short skirt revealed her shapely legs without revealing anything else.

But when she smiled at Garcia he found himself with a lump in his throat. For a moment he was an awkward schoolboy, a coltish acne fifteen, his veneer of worldliness and suaveness ripped away.

"It's good to see you again," he said quietly, with a warmth to his voice that didn't betray the turmoil within.

"It's good to see you again too. And I'm pleased to meet you, Jorme. I look forward to hearing you perform sometime."

Jorme's head bobbed awkwardly. "Thank you."

Garcia chose a wine from the bar, and Jorme followed suit.

"That's an excellent year," Shaara said approvingly. "You have good taste, Garcia."

"Surprised?"

"A little."

"I happen to appreciate the good things, Shaara, though I may not be exactly in your league."

She laughed. "When you reach a certain point, Garcia, there's not much difference, no matter how much higher you go. You're quite close to that point."

He wondered if she were toying with him, slumming, as it were, playing with a well-known musician. Was he just to be the latest conquest in a long string that perhaps included an artist, an actor, a politician, and Lord knows what else?

The room was filled with colorful people, attractive women and impressive men. A noble and elderly lady walked by, her skin still young although her hair was white. "Ah, you're Garcia." She took his hand very gently. "I've enjoyed your music *so* much."

On the far side of the room a woman in blue fur walked regally. Her belly was flat and sleek, covered with pale blue soft fur that blended gently to the glistening blue fur of her pubic area while her legs and back were fully furred with the same color. A tail, long and somewhat prehensile, protruded from her back and twitched about merrily. She delighted in tapping people on the shoulder from behind with it as she talked to them. Her breasts were firm but pale under the down fur of her front, and her ears were slightly pointed. She wore no clothing whatsoever. Garcia knew that the soles of her feet would be heavily padded. She would have to be quite rich to afford such an operation: it was costly both in time and money. The alterations were more than skin deep.

He knew all too well the expense of such surgery. He touched his right arm. It was far less expensive than the surgery that the blue-furred woman had undergone. And not much less than that which kept the white-haired woman's face young. He wondered why she didn't dye her hair. But then, perhaps, she would lose much of her regal mien. There were so many options available, options that pushed back the boundaries of aging. It wouldn't be long before the average man or woman lived a full and viable life past the age of one hundred. Many of the rich and powerful already did so.

Shaara introduced the two musicians to members of the richest and most prestigious families in the country, people who wielded power as though it were their own personal prerogative, without thought or consideration. Most of them seemed delighted to meet him and disappointed that he had not brought his autar with him. He realized that, although his name and face were better known and more easily recognized than any of theirs, it was they who had the real control of things. He was merely a plaything to them, a toy, a pawn, a court jester, a pet monkey, a prize to display as they would a painting by an old master or a sculpture or a rare recording or a fine wine.

The young scion of the Mont'Illiano family was in his late twenties, but reputedly was already in control of most of the communications net, as his father slowly removed himself from the family business.

"Garcia! A pleasure. I've enjoyed your music." Mont'Illiano's interest seemed genuine, his smile a warm one without any falseness. "I hope to see you here often. Enjoying yourself?"

"Yes, thank you," Garcia said politely, still unsure of himself in this different stratum of society, feeling his way along slowly.

"Good. We need someone here besides all these stodgy old birds without any talent except for making money."

"Monty!" Shaara admonished him.

"Well, it's true. Look at me. I can talk the birds out of the trees sometimes, especially at board meetings, but other than that, I'm useless."

Why was Shaara interested in Garcia rather than in this brash young man with whom she had so much more in common? They were both drawn from the same mold. Social parasites? Perhaps. That was the cloak they both drew over themselves, but Garcia saw something further under the surface. He had heard Mont'Illiano referred to as a bloodsucker, a leech, and it was true that he took much out of the system for his own use. Nonetheless, he put much back in. A parasite? No. A social symbiont. It would all die and wither without Mont'Illiano and his compatriots, and Garcia would die and wither with it.

The leader of the Tibaldo clan, rulers of the electromotive industry, was also young, a man in his early forties, his full head of dark hair laced with gray, steel in his smile. His gray-blue eyes seemed to pierce Garcia, taking his measure in a few swift seconds.

He moved quickly through the social amenities, and said, "This student of yours, Jorme. Is he good?" As Garcia and Shaara moved through the party, Jorme had left them, drawn into conversation with some of the younger people.

"He's quite good. You'll be hearing his name frequently very soon."

"I hope so. We need more fine musicians. You knew Bwire, didn't you?"

"I learned a great deal from him." Garcia was surprised that Tibaldo knew of Bwire, who had retired from performing more than twenty years earlier and had been out of the public eye for nearly as long.

"Artists like yourself and Bwire are rare; you're national treasures and should be treated as such."

"Put in dusty cabinets and taken out on holidays?" Garcia had tried to make the tone of his voice light, but a trace of bitterness surfaced in it nonetheless.

Tibaldo looked at him sharply. "No, that's not what I meant. But it *is* true that you should learn to pace yourself, and not burn yourself out while you're still young. You've got a long life ahead of you, probably even longer than you think. There's a lot of interesting things happening in medicine and areas like that. Get Muenstretiger to tell you about them sometime."

Jorme was flushed with excitement when he returned to Garcia's side. "This is one hell of a party! Do you know who I was talking to just a few minutes ago?"

"No." Garcia knew very well whom Jorme had been talking to.

"Pentland LaCroix!"

"The HV star?" Pentland LaCroix was the current sex symbol of the solar system.

Jorme nodded, wide-eyed.

"What did she say to you?"

"What didn't she say to me? She's something else." Jorme shook his head in wonderment. He lowered his voice. "Frankly, I think she'd like to go to bed with you."

Garcia smiled. "Well, you tell her that you have to check all my bedmates personally first. That you're my official bedmate checker."

Jorme smiled bashfully. "I couldn't do that."

Garcia put a fatherly hand on Jorme's shoulder. It seemed so strange that this awkward, shy young man could be so at home and so skillful on the autar.

He toyed with the idea of moving in on either the blue-furred woman or Pentland LaCroix. No, he thought, not Pentland. He would leave her for Jorme.

"Garcia! I heard you were here, but I couldn't believe it." The man who stood before him was vaguely familiar, as were so many of the people he had already met. But this man didn't have that now-familiar air of authority and power; instead there was something foppish about him. His clothes were those of a dandy: they were too neatly creased and folded, too sharp and meticulous. His face was chiseled out of granite: a nose too-perfect in its angularity, a chin perfectly noble, a mouth perfectly proportioned, and steel-blue eyes. Nonetheless, there was a softness to the face and a puffiness that underlay the features, already beginning to show their age. "You don't recognize me, do you?"

"No, I'm afraid not."

The other seemed delighted. "How perfect. How absolutely perfect. Practically everyone in the world knows me, recognizes me, even the powerful people in this very room, perhaps they especially, but the one person in the world whom I admire most fails to recognize me."

"I feel I *should* recognize you, but I can't quite place you."

"Jack Orion."

"Of course. I'm sorry. I should have . . ."

"No apologies, please." Orion held his hands up in an attempt to stop Garcia's apology. "I am delighted."

Perhaps Jack Orion exaggerated a bit in saying that everyone in the world would recognize him, but it wasn't a large exaggeration. He was one of the most popular commentators in the world, his sharp commentary feared by those in the public eye, from the president of the world council to the lowliest entertainer, and enjoyed by the public, especially the *barraquistes*. He had a reputation as a muckraker, and none of Garcia's friends had much use for him or much good to say about him.

"You know, I've admired you for years." Orion took Garcia by the elbow and led him toward the bar. "You've become quite a legend down in the *barraque*."

"Legends are supposed to be dead," Garcia growled, not knowing how to get away from this effusive parasite.

Orion laughed. "Well, no one thinks you're dead. In fact, there's a . . . a rumor, I guess you'd call it, or a prediction, that when you return to the *barraque* you'll lead the *barraquistes* in a revolt."

Garcia tried to echo Orion's laugh, but it was forced and unreal. "Well, there's little chance of that."

"I see you two have met." Mont'Illiano came up from behind them. "May the better man win." He had his arms around them both, like a referee between two fighters at the beginning of a match.

"It's not like that at all, Monty," Orion said. "We're not competitors. We walk in two different worlds."

"There are many levels of competition." Mont'Illiano

punched them both lightly on the shoulder, and Orion's face darkened. "Good luck to both of you. Or whatever."

"What was he talking about?" Garcia asked as the young man walked away.

"Who knows?" Orion muttered angrily. "I don't like that man, Garcia."

"Isn't he your boss, in a way?"

"Yes. He runs the communications networks, and I work for them, so I guess you could say that. But that doesn't mean I have to like him. He toys with people, Garcia; he tries to stir up trouble between them just so he can watch it. He has no respect for other people."

"He seems all right to me."

"Just wait. And watch him. This is the first time you've met him, right? The first time you've been to Muenstretiger's or any of their places?"

"Yes."

"Well, I've been with them for two years now. Ever since I got my own show. They think they're keeping an eye on me this way, I guess, but that works two ways: I'm also keeping an eye on *them*, and I'll be ready for them when the time comes. I suppose . . ." Orion thought better of whatever he was going to say. Garcia waited while the commentator took a stiff drink from his whiskey. "You know, I'm responsible for your being here tonight."

"You are?" Garcia raised an eyebrow.

Orion nodded. "I was the one who introduced Shaara to your recordings. She'd never even heard of you before that. Can you imagine?"

Garcia smiled. "There are plenty of people who have never heard of me."

"Maybe, maybe not. But the important people have. Other musicians, people who appreciate good music. And you're kind of a hero to the *barraquistes*, even though you've never been one of them. That incident a couple of years ago, the girl . . ."

"Stella Blue."

"Yes. Well, they say you've become one of them, in heart, and there are songs about you and her."

"How do you know all this?"

"It's my business. I've got contacts everywhere."

"Are you boring Garcia?" Shaara rejoined them.

"No, I'm just . . ."

"Hush." She stretched up and kissed him briefly, then took both men by the arm. "Stop being so silly."

"He wasn't boring me, Shaara."

"I don't want to hear about it."

"But . . ."

"This is a party. I don't want the two of you fighting. Will you dance with me, Garcia?"

"I'm afraid I don't dance."

"You don't? How depressing. Well, you won't mind if Jack and I do, will you?"

"No, not at all. Go ahead."

She danced away in Jack Orion's arms, laughing. "She's a strong-willed girl," a rich baritone voice said behind Garcia. It was Muenstretiger. "I really don't know how to control her." He sighed, and it seemed incongruous that such a self-controlled man should sigh. "I'm glad you're here, Garcia." He placed his hand on Garcia's shoulder. "I'm glad she likes your music. That's one thing at least that Jack Orion has done for her. She'd never heard of you before then, but that's all she talks about now. You're good. Almost as good as Bwire." Garcia wondered at the softness that stole over Muenstretiger's face, replacing the steel, and the far-off expression in his eyes.

CHAPTER 9

The party started to break up, as couples and groups began to move toward the door. "I guess I'd better be leaving," Garcia said to Shaara. "Have you seen Jorme lately?"

"Oh, the night's still young, Garcia. A bunch of us are going to The Welcome Machine. Surely you'll come along?"

"I don't know, I . . ."

"Don't be one of the old folks." Mont'Illiano slipped up behind them. "We're going to do the town. Besides, I haven't had time yet for a good talk with you. Be a good chap."

"I don't know. If Jorme . . ."

"I've already talked to him, and it's all set. All five of us will take one car, and there'll be others. Even Jack Orion." Mont'Illiano winked at Garcia. "So you see there's going to be lots of fun."

Jorme and the lovely Pentland LaCroix came up then. Jorme's face was flushed, whether with alcohol, excitement, or emotion, Garcia couldn't say. Probably all three. "Are you going to come with us, Garcia? Please do. It sounds like lots of fun."

"All right, all right."

"Excellent. Shaara, you get the limousine ready, and I'll

round up the others." Mont'Illiano moved off briskly, looking about eagerly for the other members of their party.

The entryway to The Welcome Machine was a gigantic metal maw, studded with teeth that reminded Garcia all too well of the river cleaner that had stolen his flesh-and-blood arm from him. He could hear the steady thrum and clanking of machinery behind the walls of the narrow passageway. The corridor ended on a metal mesh catwalk overlooking a cavernous room where students and artists and pseudo-artists talked, flirted, danced, drank, and occasionally listened to the music at the far end of the room.

As usual in the post-midnight hour, The Welcome Machine was full. A waiter, dressed as a robot, but in reality probably a student at the conservatory trying to make ends meet, approached them. "Five?" he asked in a tinny voice.

"There's more of us coming," Shaara said. "About twenty, all told." The robot/waiter executed a neat mechanical turn and led them to a group of tables halfway through the room.

Garcia was totally out of his element. He simply wasn't used to being surrounded by people he didn't know, strangers in grotesque costumes and eerie styles. A man walked by whose face was entirely covered by hair, only his surprisingly placid blue eyes visible, a very minor version of the type of operation the blue-furred woman had taken. Many of The Welcome Machine's customers had had minor operations of that sort—a gold-plated mechanical finger, oddly-shaped ears, small patches of various-colored fur. None of the cafe's ordinary patrons could afford a major operation, but many of them sported whatever they could afford, in an effort to proclaim their individuality.

Others, unwilling to undergo such operations for whatever reasons—lack of money or fear of undertaking something so implacably permanent—wore their hair in strange shapes, shaved their heads in erotic patterns, wore eye-jewelry and exotic clothing. Some of the women sported creatures that had been bred and created as pets, wide-eyed, fluffy mammals that scurried in and out of billowing sleeves and bouffant hairdos, staring out in fear and curiosity.

They were, thought Garcia, proclaiming themselves talented, when indeed they had no talent. It was the handful of unornamented, unmodified humans scattered throughout the club who probably were the most talented. The large man with the full red beard at a nearby table, for example, looking for all the world as countless generations of artists had looked. Was he a sculptor, perhaps, who could make a bust of Shaara that would be absolutely lifelike, then turn around and do a completely incomprehensible abstract mobile? Perhaps a scriptor for holovision or a director. Not likely to be an actor, not with such a full beard, or even a musician. A musician might settle for a small beard or a mustache, but a beard that full might get in the way.

The fake robot waiter took their orders, stood at the table a long moment, then opened the panel in his chest and delivered their drinks to them, just like an ordinary robot waiter. Garcia wondered briefly how the trick was done. Then it turned smartly in a smooth toe-heel step and moved mechanically to another table.

"Well, this wasn't quite what I had expected," Shaara said.

"What did you expect?" Garcia asked.

"I'm not sure. Something more . . . more earthy, I guess, more decadent."

Garcia smiled. "According to everything I've heard, all the decadence is mired in the, uh, the ruling classes."

Shaara scowled. "I've always wondered what the . . . the simple folk do for amusement."

"This isn't exactly the simple folk, Shaara. For that, you need to go down to the *barraque*. And that's something I wouldn't suggest you do."

"Why not? You used to go there, didn't you?"

"Yes." Garcia's voice was soft, barely audible. "Years ago. And then, only for a short time."

"And what do they do down there for enjoyment?"

"They kill themselves. Slowly, with drugs or drink, or quickly, with violence."

"I don't believe that. You're exaggerating."

"Perhaps a little. But it's no place for a lady like you. I'd stay away from there, if I were you. This is excitement enough for you."

"This," she said very emphatically, "is boring." There was an edge to her voice, of irritation and annoyance.

Like the waiters, the musicians were dressed as robots, moving in syncopated rhythms. It was a watered-down version of the *grilly* music that was very popular in the *barraque*, a discordant music with disturbing rhythms that was very difficult for a non-*barraquiste* to master. The band on the stage of The Welcome Machine was stiff, though perhaps no one in the club knew it but Garcia, who had spent several months living in the *barraque* after the death of Stella Blue. The keyboardist lacked the pedal dexterity so important to a *grilly* keyboardist. His bass was a simple

programmed thrumming, without the constantly changing
rhythms of the skilled tuntong player. The autar player
was, of course, no more than adequate. Garcia wondered if
he was a student at the conservatory. His instrument was a
quarter tone out of key.

The one saving grace of the group was its singer, a fe-
male with extraordinary range and purity, yet with the ability to growl her notes with appropriate grittiness when the
occasion required. It was that very purity, however, that
rendered her performance metallic, yes, and robotic, lacking the essence of *grilly* while attempting to elevate it beyond its basic origins.

Shaara noticed Garcia's attention to the music. "Do you
know the autar player?"

Garcia shook his head. "I know none of them. The autarist isn't very good, but the singer is quite talented."

"I wonder what she looks like under all that metal."

The trio ended to perfunctory applause; more than half
of the audience had been more involved with their own
conversations than with the music. Their place was taken
by a rather plain-looking woman who danced to recorded
music while she slowly took off her garments. Why, Garcia
wondered, should that be more erotic than the blue-furred
woman, who openly walked about naked? Only when most
of her clothes were off did Garcia realize that the woman
had a mane of bright red fur that ran down the ridge of her
spine to culminate in a short barbed tail. He grinned as
soon as he saw the tail and Shaara took him to task for it.

"Really, Garcia, I should think you would get no enjoyment out of such childish activities."

"Once upon a time, Shaara, you would have been right.

But I think it's rather cute. She should have horns and a pitchfork, however."

"That would be carrying it too far," Mont'Illiano said.

The evening continued with amateur musicians, a violinist and a guitarist playing Harrigan's Sonata for Guitar and Violin being the most accomplished. Many of the others played the computerized instruments controlled by keyboards and switches that Mars Ruby enjoyed so much.

"Where's Jack Orion?" Garcia asked. "I thought he was going to be here."

Mont'Illiano's grin was mischievous. "I, ah, gave him some misdirections, I'm afraid. He's gone somewhere else, to the Mink Julep, perhaps. I also dropped some hints that we might be going to the *barraque*."

"Oh, Monty, that's a great idea," Shaara said. "Let's go."

"I was just trying to get rid of Orion for a while. He's fun in small doses, but he does get wearisome after a while. Besides, I wanted to talk with Garcia without his distraction."

"You mean we're not going to the *barraque?*" Shaara seemed quite displeased with the thought.

"I don't think that would be a good idea."

"I'm surprised that you allow Orion to run his commentaries on HV," Garcia said. "They seem to be quite contemptuous and critical of a lot of things I should think you'd be interested in keeping as they are."

"Maintaining the status quo," Mont'Illiano said, still smiling. "But, you see, Garcia, that's exactly what we're doing."

"I'm afraid I *don't* see."

"Look, if it wasn't Orion, it'd be somebody else. But we can control *him*."

Garcia frowned. "You mean you've bought him? He sure puts on a good act."

Mont'Illiano shook his head, maintaining the grin which was beginning to irritate Garcia. "No, we're more subtle than that. What we do is feed him misinformation, not much, but a little, enough, like I did tonight to keep him away from here, and that keeps him in control, in line. We're not stupid, Garcia."

"If you're not stupid, what are you doing telling *me* all this?"

"Because, Garcia, you're one of us." As Garcia started to protest, Mont'Illiano held up his hands. "Oh, I know *you* don't think so, but you are, you will be. You'll realize that soon enough. Are you going to tell Orion about this?" Garcia shook his head. "You see?"

It was near dawn when they finally left The Welcome Machine, although the club was still more than half full and it didn't seem as if things were about to wind down. The club wouldn't shut its doors until near noon, the last of its patrons and performers struggling out from the dark recesses into the blinding light of daytime like babies leaving the womb, lost and needing only a slap to begin crying. It wouldn't open again until shortly before midnight.

Mont'Illiano offered them a ride home in his limousine, but Shaara refused, insisting that she and Garcia take an electrocab.

"Why didn't you take his offer?" Garcia asked.

"I wanted to be alone with you for a while. We haven't had a chance to be alone all night long."

Garcia smiled. "We never have." She smiled back warmly.

"Destination, please?" the voice of the driver asked through its speaker.

Garcia looked at Shaara. "What's your address?" Having taken a limousine to her estate, he had no idea what its address was.

"Do you really wish to get rid of me that easily?"

"No."

Their mutual gaze was broken when the driver repeated its question. Garcia gave the address of his apartment.

CHAPTER 10

A little before noon, although the stars still wheeled sunless overhead on Garcia's ceiling, his supervisor called his name. Garcia grumbled something and nosed back into the warmth of his bed.

"Garcia. I have Mr. Renard waiting to talk to you."

Garcia mumbled something else incomprehensible, then said in a sleep-thickened voice, "Renard? What the hell do you want?"

Renard's crisp voice, clean and unweary, replaced the supervisor's. "I've been in touch with Muenstretiger and he wants to see you this afternoon. Will three be convenient?" There was a slight edge of sarcasm to Renard's voice.

"Three? What time is it now?"

"Eleven thirty-two," the supervisor said.

"Three's okay, I guess." He looked at Shaara to confirm it, but she still had her eyes shut, although he suspected she was awake.

"He'll send a limousine over for you at three then," Renard said.

"Fine. Supe?"

"Present," the supervisor said.

"Wake me at two, will you?"

"Programmed."

Garcia turned on his side and tried to find the comfortable abyss of sleep again, not noticing that Shaara's eyes were now open and looking at him with a strange, knowing expression.

When the supervisor woke him at two, the aroma of fresh coffee filled the room, mixed with that of hot buttered toast. Shaara was no longer in bed, but he could hear the sound of water in the convenience. Then the door slid open and she came out, partially dressed, and slapped him on a naked thigh. "Hurry up, or everything will be cold!"

"Don't be silly. Those are canned smells. When will breakfast be ready, supe?"

"I can have juice and coffee for the young lady immediately, if she wants it. Your breakfast will be ready in ten minutes, as usual."

"What do you want for breakfast, Shaara?"

"What are *you* having?"

"Steak and eggs."

"Sounds wonderful. I'll have the same."

"How would you like your steak, ma'am?" the supervisor asked.

"Well done." Garcia looked at her with disappointment.

"And your eggs?"

"Let me have eggs Martian."

Garcia got off the bed, feeling the aches in his joints beginning to fade away. He had a brisk shower before breakfast.

"Your juice and coffee are ready, ma'am," he heard the supervisor say.

"Shaara," she said firmly.

"Programmed."

The liveried butler again met them at the mansion and led Garcia to a large study while Shaara went up the large stairway that led to the second floor.

Garcia walked around the room, looking at the bookcases. He had seen only a handful of actual books in his life, and he reflected that there might be more books in this room than there were on the rest of the planet.

He turned at the faint sound of a door opening on the other side of the room.

"Garcia. Glad you could come." Muenstretiger moved across the room, surely, silently, gripping Garcia's hand firmly. There was a brief moment of eye contact, then Muenstretiger broke the moment and walked over to the sideboard. "Wine?" He broke open a bottle and began pouring before Garcia could reply. He looked up, his eyes twinkling. "I understand you appreciate wine."

"Yes, sir, although I can't afford thousand-dollar bottles."

"Well, this is just a mediocre Sirency." He brought the wine over and gestured to the chairs. "I hate to rush you, but I really don't have much time, and this is going to take awhile. I think you'll be quite interested."

"Frankly, I can't see why you'd be interested in showing me anything."

Muenstretiger smiled. "Well, to tell the truth, it was my daughter's idea. But, for once, I think she's right." He pressed some buttons on his chair, the room darkened, and a holo appeared in the middle of the room, in front of them. It showed a large white laboratory rat. "How old would you say this animal was, Garcia?"

"I'm afraid I don't know very much about animals. Ten years?"

Muenstretiger raised an eyebrow. "Not bad. Actually, it's twelve years old, which is nearly four times the age at which a laboratory rat would normally die of old age. Not that many of them *do* die of old age."

"You've discovered some kind of immortal rat? I don't really care, to tell you the truth."

"No, I don't expect you to have any interest in rats. But *I* do. I run the largest pharmaceutical concern in the world, and we use a lot of rats." Muenstretiger smiled. "Some of them even work for me. But this rat is, as you have suggested, probably immortal."

"Probably?"

"Who knows when it will die? But it's not a special strain of rat, Garcia. We have obtained similar results with monkeys and pigs."

"You have monkeys and pigs working for you too?"

Muenstretiger smiled again. "You know where I'm leading, Garcia?"

"Immortality. For man."

"Not for any man, Garcia. For you."

Garcia squirmed in his chair. "I'm afraid not. I don't want to become one of your lab animals."

Muenstretiger held up a hand. "I'm not suggesting that. We've already performed the operation on several dozen human beings. It's not experimental."

"But you can't be certain it works. Not after only ten years."

"Less than that. The first operation on a human being took place a little over a year ago. Let me tell you what's involved, then you'll have a better understanding with which to make your decision."

"How much do you charge people for this experiment?"

Muenstretiger smiled. "For those who can afford it, quite a lot. But for you, Garcia, nothing. After all, you're an artistic treasure, and I feel you should receive the operation before it's too late."

An artistic treasure? Was he already carved in granite? "What do you mean, too late?"

Muenstretiger sighed. "Come on." He stood up. "I'll show you through our laboratory, and you'll understand then."

They went to a large building at the back of the estate, where they were greeted by an intense tiny man with a scraggly fringe of a beard. "This is Dr. Gregg. He'll explain the procedure to you. I'll see you later in my study."

"Ah, Garcia! A pleasure, a pleasure." Dr. Gregg pumped Garcia's hand enthusiastically. "How much has Muenstretiger explained to you?"

"Not very much, I'm afraid."

"Good. Well, I won't go into the details of how we discovered the process. Let me merely say that it was a matter of serendipity and conjecture and some brilliant leaps of logic, in which I am proud to say I had a small part, and Muenstretiger gave us his full and complete support."

"I'm sure."

"This way, please." Dr. Gregg led him to a small operating room, oblivious to Garcia's discomfort. "The first thing we do is excise a small portion of your thymus gland."

"That sounds painful."

"Oh no. We can do it without even leaving a scar." The doctor showed Garcia a small tube about a quarter of a meter in length made of clear plastic. "We merely insert this into your body, and it slides quite easily through the tissues. Then we can insert microsamplers inside it. We don't need much tissue. Come on, I'll show you."

Dr. Gregg next took Garcia to a large laboratory where technicians worked at incomprehensible tasks. "This is where we divide and culture our tissues. Over here, for example, we have those of Shaara and Mont'Illiano." The masses of tissue seemed obscene and disgusting to Garcia.

"They are going to be, uh, immortal?" he asked.

"Oh, certainly. All the major families are having their children cultured. Now, after we've cultured about twenty different samples, we send them to the Erestus facility for irradiation."

"Wouldn't that kill them or something?"

"Oh yes, we lose most of our samples that way, nearly fifty percent. And most of the others either become cancerous or mutate in unacceptable ways. But there seems to be a tendency for the immortality mutation to occur spontaneously often enough that two or three samples usually are viable for our purposes."

"And if they don't?"

Dr. Gregg shrugged. "Then we have to take another sample and try again."

"What happens after you have good samples?"

"We culture a new gland from the samples and implant it in the original donor."

"That's all there is to it?"

"Oh, there are a lot of minor details, of course." Dr. Gregg patted Garcia's stomach. "Diet, for one thing. A restricted caloric intake has always been conducive to an extended life. But that's the broad outline."

Garcia felt he was missing something important, but there was no way he could tell what it was. One of those "minor details" might, in fact, be very important.

Muenstretiger was waiting for him in the study when Dr. Gregg returned him to the main house. "Well, how do you feel about it?"

Garcia shook his head. "I feel like my head's spinning, and yet I feel I don't have all the details I need."

"Of course."

"For one thing, I still don't understand why you're offering this to *me*."

"I told you . . ."

"I know! But why not Bwire? He's much older, and he can't live much longer."

"I know. And that's the very reason why we can't help him. His body wouldn't be able to take the shock of the operations—rather than making him immortal, it would probably kill him. I'm sorry, Garcia." The industrialist was quiet for a moment then continued, almost apologetically. "You see, Shaara's mother thought a great deal of him. It was she who introduced me to his music. Bwire's music and Lupa are linked in my mind, and I wish it were possible to help him. But there's nothing we can do for him now." Muenstretiger looked at Garcia with a strange expression on his face. "So when Shaara asked me to offer it to you, his best-known pupil, it was impossible for me to say no. I hope you don't mind being my second choice."

Garcia's answer was a choked "No."

"She'll be having her own operation in about a month, as soon as her immortality gland is grown. I hope you'll agree to join us. You can help as she learns to control my organization." Muenstretiger smiled at the look on Garcia's face. "You didn't think she had that much steel in her, did you? Well, I had hoped for a son, but Shaara has proven to be the equal of any male in the business."

"No, it wasn't that." How could Garcia convey his feelings about the implicit assumption that he and Shaara would be partners? The thought had been in his own mind, but he didn't like the feeling of being herded toward it, without any say of his own in the matter. "But . . . what about you? Why should you hand over control to Shaara?"

"I won't live forever, Garcia."

"But haven't you . . . ?"

Muenstretiger shook his head. "The thymus gland atrophies after adolescence. That's the real reason why we can't help Bwire. We haven't been able to culture an immortality gland for anyone over thirty, and we haven't always been able to cultivate one for anyone over twenty-four."

"But I'm twenty-eight," Garcia protested.

Muenstretiger nodded. "That's why you should start immediately. It may already be too late for you."

CHAPTER 11

Garcia sat in his darkened apartment, looking at the screen in one wall, where the score for Tattnall's *Savannah River Suite* was projected. It would be a show piece for his opening concert in the city; it was always a favorite here. But he wondered if it would be worth continuing with it for the rest of his tour. The rushing music of its beginnings, like the headwaters of the river in the southeastern mountains, became majestic in a way that might be boring to other audiences. He would have to talk to Renard about it later. Renard had a much better feel for such things; he was more in tune with audience tastes. The agent would be surprised if Garcia asked him about it; usually, Garcia would tell him what music he planned to perform and then Renard would tell him which pieces would not be received well at certain concert sites. Then usually Garcia went ahead and performed them anyway and, more often than not, Renard would be proven right. Garcia didn't know how the agent did it, but he had a talent for predicting audiences. They would make a much better team if Garcia would listen to him more often; he resolved to do so in the future, wondering even as he made the resolution if he would be able to keep it.

Once, however, Garcia had the audience in his hands, he was usually able to flow with the energy, shaping it as he did so to his own direction and desires. It would be so much easier if he listened to Renard and played music that would get the audience and him in tune with each other much sooner.

He keyed in the music for Millen's *Weeping Willow* and practiced it for over an hour, working over the difficult passages and key changes until he had them down pat. It wasn't difficult; he hadn't played the music in over six months, but it all came back very rapidly. He decided to play a medley of *grilly* songs, beginning with the self-reflective humor of "Money Day" and ending with the mournful yet hopeful "Day Pages."

Carter's *Peanut Farm* would also be interesting, despite its local interest. It was a new addition to his repertoire. He went through it once, just to keep in practice. He had been practicing it regularly since his last concert series. Carter, although not an autar player himself, had written a moderately difficult run of thirty-second notes at the same time that the computer had to be reprogrammed three times in the space of twelve bars, including a major key change and a major change in rhythm. It had taken Garcia five months to master it to the point where he was willing to use the piece in a performance, and he prided himself on the knowledge that he was probably the only practicing autar player who was capable of performing it. Even at his peak, it might have been beyond Bwire's capabilities. Bwire himself claimed that he could never have done it, but Garcia had his doubts. The old man often played down his own ability.

They would round out the compositions that Garcia had

already told Renard he would be performing. With the other compositions, Garcia could juggle the pieces to fit the audience and his mood, and no two performances would contain the same selections unless he wanted it that way.

"Garcia, I have a call from a Mr. Jack Orion. Will you take it?"

Jack Orion? What could he want? Despite his dislike for the commentator, Garcia couldn't very well refuse the call. He'd been lucky so far. Orion had not tried to tear him down. If he offended him now . . .

"Garcia! I'm glad I caught you in." The vulpine features of Jack Orion grinned eagerly at Garcia.

"Can I help you with something, Orion?" Garcia asked cautiously.

"I don't know. I hope so." Garcia wondered whether the confusion was genuine or feigned, a trap. "There's something going on and I don't know what it is. I don't like that. I thought maybe you could help me."

"I doubt it. I don't keep in contact with much except the world of music, and I don't think that would make very good news for you."

"But you were at the party the other night, and . . . well, there was something in the air, a kind of expectancy, like they were celebrating something special."

"I didn't sense it."

Orion shook his head. "No, I guess you wouldn't. It was your first time there. But, listen, you know how we got separated after the party?"

"Yes."

"Well, you may not realize it, but it was deliberate."
Garcia tried to look quizzical. "I have my sources, and I
know that Mont'Illiano did it deliberately. He's trying to
hide something from me."

Garcia shook his head. "He didn't tell me anything that
he might want to hide from you."

Orion stared at Garcia, the air of confusion gone. "Tell
me what happened after you left me."

Garcia told Jack Orion what had happened, carefully
excising what Mont'Illiano had told him about Jack Orion.
It seemed that Orion was a bit freer than Mont'Illiano
thought.

"That's all?"

"I think I've told you everything important."

Orion worried at his lower lip with his forefinger and
thumb. "If you remember anything else, let me know."
Garcia nodded. "Or if you hear anything that might help
me. Remember, the *barraque* is counting on you, Garcia.
You're one of us."

"I'm just a musician, Orion."

Jack Orion smiled. "You're more than you think, Garcia.
Be sure to let me know if you remember anything important." He broke the connection and Garcia was left alone
with his thoughts.

He sat in the still-darkened room for a long moment,
feeling like a pawn in some game whose rules he didn't understand. Both sides claimed him as one of theirs, yet he
felt he didn't belong to either of them.

"Supervisor?"

"Yes?"

"What do you think about immortality?"

After a brief pause, the supervisor said, "Could you be more specific? What do you wish to know about immortality?"

"Do you think it's a good idea?"

"I find no value judgment attached to it. Do you speak of physical immortality or that of fame?"

"Physical immortality."

"It is a hypothetical subject. In either case, the immortality is in truth limited."

"Limited?"

"Entropy assures us that fame eventually will end, and the famous will be forgotten, since everything physical will end and all energy will become static."

"But what about longevity?"

"The oldest known human being lived to an age of one hundred and ninety-five years. He was Dewey Rose, who died in 2452. There are some alive today who may well pass that age in the near future, but the average life span is less than one hundred years, ninety-eight point seven to be precise. Extreme measures along with excellent heredity are required for longevity in excess of one hundred and twenty-five years."

"But suppose it were possible for people to live indefinitely. Would that be a wise idea?"

After a pause longer than that programmed into the supervisor, it said, "Several centuries ago Professor Michael Conrad of the University of Michigan in one of his early biological growth models accidentally included the assumption of immortality. The model stabilized at a point where no reproduction was occurring, no exploration was being made by the individual organisms into other spaces, even though those spaces were highly suitable for them. They were devoting all their resources to maintaining themselves." There was another pause. "I would not consider that to be beneficial."

CHAPTER 12

Garcia didn't see Jorme again until several days later, when they met at the auditorium where their first concert together was to be performed that night. The youngster was obviously on edge over the performance.

But Garcia had other things on his mind. He was busy tuning the auditorium.

"Is this really necessary?" Jorme asked as they entered the auditorium after conferring with the producer, Renard, and a small, red-bearded technician with whom Garcia seemed to be on close terms. "An analyzer would do a much better job, wouldn't it? How could you improve on its judgment?"

"Don't rely on machines too much." Another technician was onstage, where Jorme and Garcia would be later. Garcia activated his implanted receiver and said, "Give me a 440." The technician plucked a string on the autar. "The analyzer is a brute force device," he said to Jorme, "relying primarily on pure tones. It sets up the major tuning of an auditorium, but it's deaf to nuances."

They walked slowly around the auditorium, checking the volume of the autar's various notes. Occasionally Garcia asked for a change in the volume, but he waited until he had walked through the entire auditorium before he began to make the more delicate tuning. Then he would spend long moments at one spot, talking to the red-bearded technician, who now was at his spot with the computer at the back of the auditorium, delicately modifying the auditorium's acoustics to Garcia's specifications, while the technician onstage played different notes on the autar.

"This isn't going to do *me* any good," Jorme complained. "It's tuned to *your* instrument, not mine."

Garcia grinned. "You'll get your chance some day, don't worry." He stopped at the top of the center aisle. "Give me a little boost on the 550." The volume of the pitch began to rise. "Hold it. There. No, back it down a little. That's good. Okay. Let's hear the 440 again."

Finally Garcia was satisfied and they walked back out to the lobby, where Renard and the producer were discussing business details.

"Are you finished?" Renard asked. Garcia nodded. "Then go home and get some rest. You've got five hours to performance."

"Don't fool around with my auditorium while I'm gone."

"What do you think I am, crazy?"

As they walked to the waiting cab that the producer had provided, Jorme asked, "Do you mind if I spend the rest of the time with you?"

"You'll probably drive me crazy with your nervousness."

"I'll try not to."

"Sure." If Jorme was left to himself, he would probably be a nervous wreck by concert time. Garcia would have preferred to be alone but the necessity of calming Jorme was one more cross he had to bear, now that he was a teacher.

But Jorme's mind was on other things. The cab had barely begun its journey through the streets to Garcia's apartment when the young autarist blurted out, "What do you think of Pentland LaCroix?"

Ah-ha! Garcia grinned. "So! That's why I saw so little of you the other night." Jorme's face turned beet-red. "Is she as good in bed as she is to look at?"

Jorme shook his head. "I couldn't talk about things like that."

"Always the gentleman, eh?" Jorme was silent. "So just what is it you want me to say?"

"I don't know. It's all so confusing."

Garcia sighed. It was incredible that Jorme should be so innocent and naïve. He wondered if Bwire had considered that when he sent Jorme to him. If Jorme had been as Garcia had when he was still a student at the conservatory, there would have been instant friction between them. They would have been competitors and rivals, not the teacher and his protégé they had so easily become.

He wondered if he should exchange intimacy for intimacy and tell Jorme about the immortality offer. As Pentland LaCroix had been disturbing Jorme, the immortality offer had been disturbing Garcia. It was a strong temptation, yet for some reason it disturbed him. It had stirred up the emotions that had begun to coalesce and destroyed whatever pattern had been forming. He was twenty-eight years old, by no means an old man, but not exactly young either. His mortality was beginning to lie on him, not heavy yet, but perceptible. Death was a long way off, but for the first time he could see it, and the years between suddenly seemed so few. The approaching end of Bwire's life only sharpened that awareness.

When they reached Garcia's apartment, Garcia poured out some wine. He sipped it meditatively while Jorme drank it in large gulps. "Not too much now," Garcia cautioned as he poured a second glass for Jorme. "You don't want to be drunk for tonight's performance."

"I don't? I'm so nervous I don't think I could even hold an autar, much less play one. I might do better if I was so drunk I didn't care."

"Nonsense. You've been through this before."

"No." Jorme shook his head emphatically. "No, I haven't. I have never before performed on the same stage as Garcia. I'm afraid they'll boo me off the platform."

"Don't worry about it."

"Don't worry about it, don't worry about it. How can I *not* worry about it?" Jorme began to pace the room, his large ungainly hands moving incessantly.

"Think about something else."

"What?"

"I don't know . . . Wait a minute." Garcia went to his tape library, finally choosing a cassette that didn't seem to match any of the others in the library. He inserted it into the flat television and turned it on.

"What is it?" Jorme asked.

The screen lit up and they were looking at an old man . . . not as old as Bwire but older than Garcia . . . playing a very early model autar. The playing was ragged and imprecise; even the most inept student at the conservatory could do better—but his playing possessed a power and a strength that surpassed that of Jorme or Garcia.

"Who is it?" Jorme asked in a low intense whisper, as if the autarist on the tape could hear him and be interrupted.

"Radcliffe."

"How . . . ?"

"It was one of Stella Blue's possessions. She left it to me."

A man grown old and haggard before his time played on an ancient autar. His technique was clumsy and simplistic, but there was a raw power that could not be denied. When he was finished, the audience that had been watching him applauded for a long time. He stood before them, his gray-streaked head bowed. The camera moved closer, and Garcia and Jorme could see the lines, the crow's-feet, the despair.

The screen grew dark. "That was his last concert." Garcia's voice was soft and subdued. "The film was taken by one of the time-dippers."

"Stella Blue?" Jorme's voice was almost a whisper. Garcia understood. There was something in Radcliffe's performance that was monumental and timeless, immortal, despite its simplicity. Or, perhaps, because of it.

"No. She had been cashiered out by then, because of her involvement with him. One of her friends took the film for her."

Jorme shook his head. "God. I wish I could play like that."

Garcia smiled. "So do I, Jorme. So do I."

CHAPTER 13

Jorme's nervousness disappeared when they reached the auditorium. But it was not replaced with an easy acceptance of the situation; instead he became a stiff, wooden zombie. Garcia's own nervousness before a performance, which he refused to admit even existed, was heightened by his concern for Jorme: if Garcia was nervous, Jorme was absolutely frightened. Even Pentland LaCroix was unable to do anything, and they both watched helplessly from the stage wings as the youngster finally walked out in front of the audience.

By the time he sat down on the stage with his instrument, however, all traces of nervousness had sloughed off him, and Jorme seemed as calm and composed as if he were playing in his own room. He was wearing garments of an identical cut to those of Garcia, although his were of a deep blue while Garcia's were a dark wine in color.

Jorme touched the autar and began his performance with Dark's *Elysian Visions*. For the next forty minutes Garcia empathized with each semiquaver out of pitch, with each slightly-ragged tempo. But, if the performance lacked the precision that Garcia could have desired, it had enough power and strength to steamroller over most objections. Jorme need make apologies to no one.

At last, the performance over, Jorme took his bows and

walked calmly offstage, his garments dripping with sweat, to receive Garcia's embrace. "Marvelous, Jorme, simply marvelous. See? You didn't have anything to worry about."

"None of us back here were worried," Renard said sardonically.

"God! I thought it would never end. Did you hear that flub in the third movement of the 'Danbury' Sonata?"

"You covered well. Only a handful of people would have noticed it. Maybe only you and me."

Jorme looked at Garcia quizzically. "Isn't that enough?" He looked around. "Is there something to drink back here? I'm dying of thirst." A stagehand thrust a container of liquid in his hand. It contained minerals and salts to replenish those that Jorme had lost. He took a long drink from it, then turned to Garcia, grinning. "You're next."

During the intermission Garcia called Bwire. "Did you catch Jorme's performance?"

"Excellent. He's definitely improved his technique under you, Garcia. That little thing he did in the 'Danbury' Sonata reminded me of one of *your* early concerts." Garcia felt himself blushing. "You're an excellent teacher."

"More than that. His attitude is changing." Garcia told him about the brief interchange backstage when Jorme's performance was over. Bwire smiled. "Would you like to congratulate him?"

"Certainly."

While Jorme talked to the old master, Garcia wondered whether or not he should tell Bwire about the immortality offer. Now wasn't the time, of course; he would have to wait until he was alone with Bwire. But wouldn't it be cruel to tell Bwire that he'd been granted immortality when Bwire himself was so close to death?

Garcia walked back to the terminal when Jorme beckoned to him.

"I have been thinking, Garcia." Bwire paused and looked at him shrewdly. "My transcription of the Harrigan sonata seems to be lacking. I've made a few notes. I'll send them over to you. I'd like you to patch it up for me."

"The sonata is brilliant, Bwire!" Garcia objected.

"Nonetheless, I have a few ideas for making it more brilliant. I'd like you to look at them."

Garcia agreed to do so, then broke the connection.

"Maybe you ought to do some transcriptions of your own," Jorme suggested.

"I'm not a composer," Garcia growled. "Performing's enough work as it is."

"I thought you enjoyed performing."

Garcia punched Jorme playfully on the shoulder. "Do you have to pick up on every contradiction I make?"

"Five minutes," Renard said.

Garcia uncased his autar and powered it up, checked the tuning, and began running scales and exercises, flexing his fingers. The producer looked at him when he paused and Garcia nodded.

"Two minutes," the producer said. The houselights dimmed slowly and brightened back up several times, and the audience began to filter back into the house.

"Who's running the show tonight?" Garcia asked.

"Steinbrunner," the producer replied.

Garcia smiled. "He's a good man."

"The best."

In a booth at the back of the auditorium, the red-bearded technician Steinbrunner was running the computer that controlled the lights, the sets, the sound, and everything else associated with the technical end of the theater. The holocameras that were mounted discreetly in the ceiling and in small boxes in the footlights would be controlled by the technician, although the final transmissions would be determined by the producer. Like Garcia, Steinbrunner was a perfectionist, disgruntled whenever he made the slightest mistake, even though no one but he might know the difference.

The producer signaled to Garcia and he walked out onto the stage. The spotlight caught him a millisecond after he emerged from the wings and followed him faithfully to the comfortable chair at center stage.

Despite what he told Jorme and everyone else, Garcia always was nervous before a performance, although he usually was unaware of it himself. There was a warmth in his chest, a fear, and he became unusually animated so that Renard was always trying to calm him down. The first few moments of the performance were always the most fretful.

While the applause was dying, Garcia checked his tuning once more, then began a slow moody piece which gradually accelerated until there was an eight-bar arpeggio central section. Meanwhile, the computer backed him with a syncopated rhythm and chords in associated minors. As he moved into the arpeggio section, he reset the computer to a simple rhythm then back again as the music died.

Meanwhile the white spotlight which had engulfed him slowly faded while a soft blue haze from the stage lights rose until he was surrounded in a blue that turned metallic in the arpeggio section. The crossfade was done flawlessly and imperceptibly, and when the piece was finished Garcia was bathed in an intense blue-white.

He followed with one of Bwire's transcriptions of a minor twentieth-century composer, a brief composition of Arca's, and then changed the mood with a medley of *grilly* tunes. The computer picked up a harsh edge, stumbling as it tried to follow Garcia's rapid tempo changes. The stumbles were not accidental, but it took an accomplished autarist to keep the computer that confused, without losing the rhythm entirely. To prove that it was not accidental, Garcia ran through the changes three times, producing the exact same stumble each time.

Steinbrunner followed Garcia's performance with appropriate lighting, the *grilly* medley accompanied by constantly changing swirls of color, predominantly yellows and reds.

The *grilly* medley brought the audience to its feet, even before he was finished, shouting and yelling. A few of the younger people tried to dance to the music.

The final piece was Bwire's *Wine* variations, a long sonata whose mood changed from the bubbliness of champagne to the deep moodiness of a rich burgundy. Steinbrunner's lighting followed the mood, with claret shades predominant. Garcia had pushed himself quite far during the *Wine* variations, so he settled for a very simple and straightforward encore.

He could still hear their applause when he finally left the stage unwillingly, not wanting to come back to the mundane world, barely feeling Renard's hand on his arm, hearing the congratulations and the words, but unable to make any sense of them. He was guided to the backstage couch, and a glass placed in his hand and practically guided to his mouth.

"Brilliant, Garcia. I swear, every time I think you can go no further, and yet you keep surpassing yourself." It was Mars Ruby. How much longer could he surpass himself? How long would it be before he merely rested on his reputation?

"Steinbrunner," he said, in a voice that was surprisingly thick. "Where is he?"

The producer smiled. "You won't see him tonight, Garcia. You know that."

Garcia nodded. The little red-bearded technician rarely came backstage after a performance. He was rarely seen even during rehearsals. He stayed in his tiny room at the back of the auditorium, watching his dials and controls, guiding his computer through its intricate paces. When the theater was empty, he would come out to move the lights and other stage pieces where he wanted them, where the theater machinery could locate them and aim them precisely.

Was he up there even now, waiting for everyone to leave, so he could be alone with his theater mistress? Or had he already slipped out through his private entrance, mingling with the departing audience, unseen and unnoticed? And yet without his artistry and craft, the performance would have had much less impact.

The whole theater and performing world sometimes seemed to be a world of freaks and cripples: Garcia himself, so isolated in his apartment, isolated from reality throughout his whole life, so that when he had met Stella

Blue, his defenses were barely formed; Jorme, so shy and insecure, and yet in a way much more worldly than Garcia had been at his age or perhaps was even now, a working-man's son, without the knowledge of the social graces so necessary in the circles where Garcia moved, and yet so cognizant of the large world outside those circles; Mars Ruby, courtesan of the arts, a moderately-talented librettist herself, who nonetheless was best known for her bedroom liaisons with famous artists; Renard, a man who trusted no one and yet wanted to trust someone so desperately, but afraid to do so, sour and sarcastic, building walls between himself and those who could become close to him; Justin Mead and his wife, both musicians with no common ground on which they could meet, performing different types of music and trying to destroy each other, yet unwilling to separate; and poor Philip Steinbrunner, an enigma in the shell of his control room, a solitary figure whose only mistress and lover was the theater itself.

Garcia's reverie was broken by a call from Bwire. "Excellent," the old master said. "You improve every time, Garcia. It was a new composition you played tonight; it wasn't what I thought I had written."

"I played every note in your score," Garcia protested.

Bwire smiled. "You misinterpret me. You played what I wrote and more. You reached beyond me, and I appreciate it."

Garcia shook his head. "I didn't add anything to it. It was everything you wrote; it was there in the score."

"Perhaps you should compose something yourself, Garcia. Then you would know what I mean, when you heard someone else play it."

Garcia regained his composure and smiled at the old man. "I'm not a composer, Bwire."

"Why not? You have all the knowledge, and more than most composers. No matter. I have to get my beauty sleep. Convey my congratulations once more to Jorme. He has a good teacher, and I'm proud of both of you."

"Thank you, Bwire."

Garcia stood there for a moment, thinking that he and Jorme were more children and family to Bwire than his own flesh-and-blood daughter, who knew nothing about music and cared less.

"What are you standing around for?" Renard asked. "It's time for a party."

CHAPTER 14

Garcia would have preferred to stay where he was, performing in his own familiar auditorium instead of traveling from city to city for several weeks. Although he wasn't paranoid about the transplats, they still made him nervous after all these years. He had never been able to verify any of the stories about people coming out of the transplat all scrambled: they were apocryphal, the stuff of nightmares and childhood terrors. Nonetheless, he distrusted the machines.

Some people claimed they felt a moment of disorienting darkness in the transmission interval, ghosts passing at light speeds through optic fibers, crosstalking to each other, but Garcia had never felt a thing. He just walked into the booth and sat there a few moments, watching the warning light turn red, warning him not to leave the booth, then quickly turn green again. When he left the booth there would be a different attendant, and the city outside the doors of the transplat terminal would be different. It would be nice if he left it slim and slender and suave, but that was even less likely than coming out scrambled. Things were best as they were.

When he had been Jorme's age, he had enjoyed the travel, exploring each city eagerly, if a bit superficially, but now they had all become the same, and the joy and taste of each was gone. Each had its own version of the *barraque*, its rich section, its artistic bohemian quarter, its business section (where the auditoriums usually were located) and its sections where the middle-incomers and the rising well-to-do lived. The details changed from city to city, but after a while they all merged into one featureless blur. Better to get to know one city well than to sample a little of each but never get to know any of them deeply.

Even the auditoriums, once the central focus of his existence, were beginning to merge, until he was astonished that the details of Casablanca were not found in Madrid, when the remaining oriental features of Hong Kong and Tokyo surprised him.

Jorme, on the other hand, was eager to explore Paris, the site of their next concert. Was it possible that he had never left the confines of his own city? Jorme blushed and admitted that he had only been out of the city twice, and then only for a short time.

"Where did you go?" Garcia asked.

"The Rocky Mountain park. Have you ever been there?"

Garcia shook his head. "No. To tell the truth, I've never been out of the city complexes."

Jorme regarded him oddly. "Haven't you ever had any desire to visit the parks?"

"No. Why should I?"

"Just to experience them. They're so different from the cities. You can't imagine what they're like."

"Breathing raw air and far from the nearest convenience? No thanks."

"You don't know how exhilarating raw air can be. And the conveniences aren't *that* far away. They're no further away than they are in the *barraques*."

"I've been through that once, Jorme. Not again."

Nonetheless he went with Jorme through the ancient city, which was now more museum than city, to the fabled Antoine's, where traditional ancient musicians played traditional ancient music on traditional ancient instruments, raw and full of impure tones, the harmonics from the horns grating on the ear. Even Jorme complained that the music was painful to listen to.

"Once all music was that way," Garcia said. "Even the original autars didn't play as precisely as we're used to. There were lots of spurious harmonics."

"How could they stand it?"

"They thought it was beautiful."

Jorme shook his head sadly.

After dinner they strolled through Montmartre and the artists' quarter, apparently unchanged for a thousand years, although they both knew that most of the buildings had been recreated from old photographs and prints: they stopped for coffee at the Louvre, where artists hawked prints of the Eiffel Tower, the Statue of Liberty, and Notre Dame; they walked through the Tuileries, the Bastille, and Versailles, all recreated from their most flowering periods; they watched fandango dancers and apache dancers on the streets of the Left Bank.

Shaara was waiting for Garcia in his room when they returned to their hotel.

"What are you doing here?" he asked.

"Renard let me in." She smiled coquettishly.

He smiled back, pleased and strangely touched. "I wish I'd known you were coming. I hope you didn't wait long."

"Oh, that's all right. I enjoyed it."

She moved toward him and, for a long moment, there were no more words between them.

"You know, you act toward Jorme like a father, and you're not even thirty years old yet."

"Do I?" The thought bothered Garcia, and yet it also had a kind of charm to it.

"Yes. You're not like that with other musicians, are you?"

"Hardly. I've always been kind of separate, even at the conservatory. Other kinds of musicians, like Justin Mead, didn't bother me. But I didn't like being near other autarists."

"Competition?"

"Maybe. I'm not sure."

"They must have thought you were some kind of a snot."

Garcia grimaced. "Yeah. I guess they did."

"But you were better than any of them, weren't you?"

"Not when I started, I wasn't. I mean, I was younger than anyone else, but I still had a lot to learn. I guess I *was* kind of a snot, though. I thought it was going to be easy."

"Was it?"

"Most of it was." Perhaps that was the trouble. Perhaps it had all come *too* easy. He had come to the end of the road, and there were no challenges left, no new roads to conquer.

They lay there together for a long moment, slowly caressing each other.

Pentland LaCroix joined them in Rome, and the two couples toured the ancient city together. Although it was far older than Paris, it was still alive and full of people, not a museum, an epitaph to the past, as Paris had become. The old buildings of the Roman Empire, the Coliseum, the viaducts, all the buildings that had stood for two thousand years, were worn and eroded by the acid rains and the polluted air of the twentieth century. All that remained of the Coliseum was a small bank of seats, now encased in a hermetic block of glassite, to be viewed but not touched. Nearby, a four-foot-diameter model showed what the Coliseum had looked like in its prime.

"It's sad, in a way, you know?" Pentland said. "All the great buildings of the past are gone."

"We have their reconstructions," Garcia said.

"It's not the same." Pentland stared moodily at the model. "Think what it must have been like to stand in the center of the Coliseum with thousands of people around you, *thousands*, in the flesh, to cheer you while you performed."

"Or boo you, or throw vegetables or worse."

"Besides," Jorme said, "they didn't perform at the Coliseum. They were sacrificed or fed to the lions."

"And the Globe Theater," Pentland continued, her eyes focused on some distant dream.

"The what?" Garcia asked.

"The Globe Theater. Where Shakespeare performed."

"Oh."

"Is that in Rome?" Garcia asked.

"You guys!" Pentland's mouth was twisted into a wry smile. "You don't have any culture."

But it *was* sad, to think of those buildings that had survived so long and yet had succumbed so rapidly to civilization. How many generations separated Garcia from Julius Caesar? Hundreds. If Julius Caesar were alive today, would he weep for the vanished Coliseum? Or would he just build another of the day's evanescent buildings? The auditorium where Garcia performed would someday be gone, just like the Coliseum. It probably would not last nearly as long.

In Hong Kong, Garcia found himself alone with Pentland LaCroix for a few moments. They had spent so much time together, Jorme and Pentland, Garcia and Shaara, young lovers enjoying the cities, enjoying themselves, a double cocoon over them, friends and lovers. Frequently the two couples would separate and, as has happened since time immemorial, the two men and the two women would be alone together. But rarely had Garcia been alone with Pentland.

"Sometimes," she said, "you seem so aloof, as though you're somewhere else."

"I've never been very good at being with people." He found it hard to look her in the eye.

She smiled. "I didn't notice that at Muenstretiger's, or after your concerts."

"Parties are different. I can perform there, but being

alone with people, with friends, is a different thing and I don't always know how to act. Besides, you're all so much younger than me."

"Five years." Pentland cocked her head at him. "You're not an old man, Garcia."

"No, but you and Shaara and Jorme are all pretty much the same age and, well, I just find it hard to feel like I'm one with you all, sometimes."

"Garcia!" She covered his hand with her slender one. "You *are* one of us, and you certainly are not old." But already there were gray hairs. Was that a bad omen? Would his immortality gland not be viable? He dared say nothing to Shaara or to Muenstretiger.

"There you are! Stealing my girl, are you?" Jorme and Shaara came around the corner of the building, carrying presents for Garcia and Pentland.

When they reached Nairobi for the last week of concerts, Shaara said, "This will be the last concert I'll be able to attend."

"What?"

"It's time for my operation. I've got to leave tomorrow morning."

"When will . . . ?" He stopped.

"I'll probably still be in the hospital when you return. You'll come to visit me, won't you?"

"Of course."

His performance that night was even more moving than usual, a blend of joy, sadness, expectation, and doubt. He added the Radcliffe sonata for the first time during the

tour, his mind full of the young girl who had truly intro-
duced him to the inventor of the autar. The technician at
Nairobi was no Steinbrunner, but he was competent, and
Garcia was able to fill the hall with his emotions.

CHAPTER 15

The final concert of their tour was to be in their home city again. Garcia had paid little attention to the critics during the tour, although Jorme came to him with each little carp and cavil, each praise and adulation. Most of the praise was for Garcia, although every two-bit critic had to find some fault, however minor, with his performance. Jorme had not fared as well, but most of the critics were kind, content to damn him with such faint praise as, "In time, Jorme will be in the same class as his teacher."

Jorme took the criticism hard, as Garcia had been afraid he would, but he managed to perform credibly nonetheless, and Garcia was certain that in time he would be as inured to the critics as Garcia had become. There was only one critic to whom Garcia ever listened, the academician Elnor, who had been disappointed by the change in Garcia's style after the death of Stella Blue. Elnor's obsession, as Garcia's had once been, was technique and precision. He could not deny Garcia's still crisp technique, but he did not understand the passion. Garcia was afraid that he would tear poor Jorme to bits, for Jorme's forte was power and passion, although his technique improved with each performance.

Elnor apparently had not attended the first concert, for

there had been no review from him. Perhaps he was saving himself for the final concert.

Garcia had heard nothing from Shaara during the last two concerts and, despite her assurances, he was worried. He fidgeted all the time, unwilling to make a panic call while Jorme and Renard were around. But as soon as he was alone he placed a call to Muenstretiger's residence. After passing through three levels of servants and secretaries, he finally found himself face to face with the industrialist.

"Ah, yes. Garcia. Have you decided to accept our offer?"

"Certainly. I'll undergo the first operation as soon as my final concert is over. But that's not why I called you."

"You'd like to talk to my daughter."

"Yes."

"I'll have her contact you as soon as possible."

"When will that be?" Garcia's panic and worry rose even further; were there some complications with her operation?

"Oh, it shouldn't be long. I'll have one of my men contact her and she should call you back within the hour. Probably less. Hang on." Garcia watched while Muenstretiger talked to one of his subordinates on another line. He turned back to Garcia, smiling. "All right. Let me put you in contact with DeLuc. He'll make an appointment for the first operation."

A few seconds later one of Muenstretiger's subordinates appeared and Garcia made an appointment for the day after his final concert. "We'll send a limousine for you," the subordinate said, and broke the contact.

Garcia stared at the now-empty room, unseeing. Was

that all there was to it? Was it that simple to become immortal? No, that was just the start. But with a few simple
words he had committed himself to the whole process.
How easy it was to change the whole course of your life,
not even knowing if it was the right thing to do.

Why . . . *why* did he feel so uneasy about accepting
Muenstretiger's offer? He should have jumped at it. Instead he kept coming up with excuses for delaying the
process and avoiding it. Perhaps in a couple of years. But
by then it might already be too late; his thymus gland
would be gone, absorbed by his body and his chance at immortality forever departed.

There was a soft chime and the supervisor announced
Shaara's call.

"Garcia! You're back." There was no projected image in
the middle of the room.

"Shaara. Where are you? Let me see you."

"No. Not yet. Not in bed." Did he detect an edge of
panic, of fear, in her voice? "Not in a hospital bed." She
laughed briefly and it sounded hollow and brittle to Garcia's ears.

"Oh, come now." He found his attempt at joviality to be
an effort. "You can't look that bad. Where are you?"

"Infants Grove. But you can't come to see me, Garcia."

"Why not? The operation hasn't changed your appearance, has it?"

"No, but . . . it's very cosely guarded. You understand,
don't you?"

"No, I don't!" It was the closest they'd yet come to having an argument. "Look, Shaara, I love you."

"You love a lot of women."

"Not the way I love you. Why can't I see you now?"

"Because, darling, I've just had an operation and the danger of sickness and contagion is . . ."

"Damn it, girl, that kind of thing was conquered long ago!"

"But we immortals don't take unnecessary chances. There's no sense in taking chances, however slight, with the loss of eternity at stake."

"Okay," Garcia grumbled.

"I've got to stop now, dear. Time for my beauty sleep. I'll watch your last concert on HV."

"Okay."

Garcia stared at the empty room, seeming emptier without even her voice. Was he that far gone? What was she? A rich man's daughter, with apparently mediocre talents. There were so many other more interesting and talented women who would be eager to share his life. His *life!* This wasn't for a few nights or even a few years, but a lifetime. And his life would stretch out into an unending future.

Of course, that was ridiculous. It wasn't immortality they were talking about. Sooner or later, all these so-called "immortals" would die. But how long, how long, into the interminable future before that day would come? So it was natural, perhaps, that they would take extraordinary measures against disease and accidental death. But it bothered him.

The supervisor chimed again, announcing a call from Jack Orion. Garcia hesitated before allowing the supervisor to complete the connection, but he felt he really had no choice. If Orion even so much as suspected what Garcia knew . . .

"Have you found out anything, Garcia?"

"About what?" Garcia let his uneasiness surface in irritation. That should be a safe emotion.

"I don't know what, but I'll find out, damn it. Listen, it has something to do with Muenstretiger. He's very important, and you're very close to him now, aren't you?"

"I've seen him only briefly since the party. I spend most of my time with Shaara, not with him."

Jack Orion was quiet for a long moment, and Garcia wondered what calculations were going on behind those shrewd eyes. "Yes, you've been seeing a lot of her, haven't you?"

"Yea, I have. What of it? We like each other."

"Garcia, she's one of *them*. Her father is grooming her to take his place when he dies."

"Yes. He's already told me that."

Orion's eyes seemed to pierce Garcia. "And where does that leave you? When she takes over his position, what will you do?"

Garcia sighed. "I'll cross that bridge when I come to it. I'm not an industrialist, Orion, I'm a musician. What Shaara does or doesn't do is no concern of mine."

Orion raised an eyebrow theatrically. "No? I'd say otherwise. Nonetheless, I'm expecting you to let me know if you learn anything important."

"Listen, Orion, neither you nor Shaara nor Muenstretiger nor anyone else own me. I don't have to take any veiled threats from you or anyone else."

To Garcia's surprise, the commentator backed off. "I didn't mean to threaten you, Garcia." His tone was oily and placating. "I'm just reminding you. I don't have any power, Garcia." Garcia thought otherwise but said nothing. "Well, if you have nothing to tell me, I'll leave you alone. But I hope you'll think over what I've said and please don't hold anything back. We're all counting on you."

Garcia stared at the empty holostage, both hands, artificial and real, clenched into useless fists.

CHAPTER 16

Bwire appeared more withered and sere than he had just a few weeks earlier, as though he had aged years in that short time. If ever there was a reason for Garcia to accept the offer of immortality, it was sitting in front of him. And yet Garcia felt guilty that Bwire would never know immortality.

His skin was the color of old suede, mottled and dull leathery tan, and he did not rise from the chair but motioned weakly toward the chair opposite. As before, the nurse outside the room, monitoring the old master, had warned Garcia not to get him excited, that they could spend only a few minutes together.

"How are you feeling?" Garcia asked awkwardly.

"As well as could be expected. I'll live to see your concert tomorrow. I expect to enjoy it." The words were delivered almost as an ultimatum: I'd *better* enjoy it, the old man seemed to say, if you know what's good for you.

"Your nurse said I couldn't stay with you very long."

"I know, I know." Bwire waved a hand peevishly. "They say not to get excited, then they do all they can to cause you to get exasperated and frustrated." Garcia waited, not knowing what to say. "Over there, over there." Bwire pointed to the cabinet on the far side of the room. "There are some papers. Bring them here."

Garcia walked over to the cabinet, finding a sheaf of music paper with notes scrawled over them. "These?"

"Yes. Bring them here." Garcia did. "This is my Sonata for Autar and Flute. For you and Justin. It needs work. I want you to finish it."

"But . . . I can't do that."

"Who else?"

"I don't know anything about composing."

"Nonsense. You know more about music than most composers." Bwire looked up at Garcia, and the harsh brown eyes seemed to soften. "Please," he said in a voice so gentle it pierced Garcia like an arrow made of neutrinos.

"I . . . I . . ." Bwire smiled at Garcia's uncharacteristic lack of words. "Why don't you keep it for now," Garcia said finally, "and I'll finish it for you when . . . if . . ."

"When I die," Bwire said calmly. "Face it, my friend. I have. Long ago."

"How can you . . . ?"

"How can I not?" Bwire spread his hands in a gesture of resignation. "You saw how I was, a couple of years ago. Frantic, frightened."

"No!"

"Yes. I was. Now. As you say, our time is limited. I accept your offer. But let us go over the score. Here. Can you read my scribbles?"

"Of course." Garcia had read Bwire's "scribbles" too many times in the past and, though the master's hand was shaky, it was still legible.

"Now. I wanted to make a more intricate pattern for the computer here, but I wasn't certain it could be programmed fast enough."

Garcia looked where the skeletal finger pointed. While the autarist was playing a series of arpeggios, and the flute was soaring over the accompaniment in long glissandos, the computer's harmonics required a change in programming as the key altered through a series of sixth slides.

"Maybe if we let the computer do the sixths rather than the autar," Garcia suggested.

"I thought of that. But there would be a gap in the texture if the autarist was silent during the change."

"But if we preprogrammed the key change and activated that key change one string at a time, it would be possible to play single notes and two- or three-note chords on the open strings as the key changed, and stay in tune with the computer."

"Interesting. It could be done?"

"I think so."

"All right. Let's change the melody line for the performer then, and let the computer handle the key change."

They worked together for nearly an hour, despite several interruptions from Bwire's nurse, who kept insisting that it was time for Garcia to leave. Each time Bwire waved her away, until at last she refused to take no for an answer.

Garcia looked at the closed door, wondering if he would ever see Bwire alive again. He kept wondering that each time he saw him, and one day it would happen. Would it be this time? He had wanted to talk to the nurse, find out how badly off Bwire really was, but she had stayed inside with him, shutting the door to any inquiry.

Goodbye. Sometimes it seemed that life was nothing but a constant series of goodbyes. And how many more, how infinitely many more goodbyes there would be if he were immortal. He had told no one, not Bwire, not Jorme, not Justin, not even Mars Ruby or Renard, about Muenstretiger's offer. How could he? He felt ashamed of being singled out, and he didn't want to hear their false congratulations and see the envy and jealousy behind their masks. Bwire alone might understand and not be jealous . . . but Garcia did not have the heart to tell him. Bwire would never know; Garcia was determined of that.

CHAPTER 17

Garcia didn't see Jorme after they returned home until they met again for the final concert at the same auditorium where they had begun. It was a different Jorme that Garcia met, different from the Jorme who had been so nervous before his first concert with Garcia. It was the eager, puppyish Jorme with whom Garcia was so familiar that now showed up at the auditorium.

"You'll never guess what I did yesterday!" he announced as soon as he saw Garcia.

"What did you do yesterday?" Garcia knew, for Bwire had already told him.

"I went to the conservatory and, Garcia, it was incredible. They treated me like some kind of conquering hero."

"Well, you've put on quite a series of concerts. You've conquered the public, and you've got a reputation now that can't help but grow."

"Well, it wasn't only me." The puppy exuberance turned into an awkward shyness. "Pentland was with me too."

Garcia thought of berating the youngster for not showing up for the auditorium tuning that afternoon but decided to say nothing. He had accompanied Garcia to every other auditorium when it was tuned, and it must have become as boring to him as it had to Garcia when Bwire had shown him how to tune an auditorium.

Jorme was eager for his last performance, and he practically swaggered out onto the stage. The tour had definitely been good for his confidence. Even if he had received no rave reviews, at least most of them had been kind, and no one had chopped him to pieces. And several times he had been called back for second encores.

Tonight he would be performing Bishop's transcription of Ohana's Concerto for Guitar and Orchestra, the computer performing percussive effects with remarkable fidelity to the original. It would be the sum total of Jorme's final performance, except for the encores. Garcia watched from the wings, half nervous, half proud, grinning, sneaking glimpses at the monitor from time to time but keeping most of his attention on the live performance itself.

Pentland LaCroix was at his side, as nervous and proud as Garcia, and they exchanged only a few words, rapt in the youngster's performance. But Garcia was constantly aware of her presence. She wasn't the fluff-headed beautiful woman he originally had assumed her to be. There was a sharp mind behind those good looks, and a gentle human being, whose edges hadn't been honed to sharp points by the media and the pressures of the holovision world. If she could maintain her balance, she and Jorme might make a good pair.

Matchmaker! Now Garcia's smile was for himself. He was thinking about Jorme as though Jorme were his son, much in the same manner that Bwire treated Garcia.

Jorme finished a nearly flawless performance of the con-

certo and was called back for a second encore. Garcia
hoped they would call him back for one more, but the audience quieted down as soon as he finished the second one
and began moving toward the lobby for the intermission.

Meanwhile the tension mounted in Garcia. He took the
customary call from Bwire, talked with Jorme, congrat-
ulating him, checked the tuning of his autar and rechecked
it, until finally the audience returned and he walked out on
the stage again, calmness settling over him like a cloak.

Unlike Jorme, Garcia had chosen a series of brief pieces
rather than one long one, terminating in Carter's *Peanut
Farm*, which he had mastered still further on the tour, although there were a few passages he wasn't satisfied with
yet. But it was strange how a piece that he performed so
well and competently at home while practicing suddenly
became alive and electric during a performance, a whole
new piece with a life of its own. No, he wasn't like Jorme:
he needed the crowds, the audience, the performance itself.
This was when he felt most alive, emotions pulsing
through him like electrical currents, his thoughts as swift
and piercing as the calculations of any computer, his per-
ceptions heightened until it seemed every note took on a
crispness and brilliance that could never be equaled again.
But there was the next one, as crisp and as brilliant.

This was what he lived for, this was his reason for existence. And yet . . . though the joy and excitement of performing were there and as sharp as ever (somehow subtly
forgotten during the months when he didn't perform),
there was a nagging doubt at the back of his mind. Was
this really all there was to life? Wasn't there something

else, besides performing someone else's compositions, re-creating, in effect, someone else's emotions? While his mind was caught in the questions, his fingers performed like separate creatures until the concert was over, and it seemed it had barely begun.

It was all so anticlimactic, such a tremendous letdown, to be finished with performing once again. All the electricity, all the anticipation, and what was left? Nothing. A handful of tapes, a mindful of memories that would fade in time. And the cycle would be repeated again in another few months, and again, and yet again, for how long?

If he were immortal, he would have time for uncounted careers. He could become a physicist or an astronomer. Or could he? The autar had been his life since he was seven years old. Would it in time become boring? Would he reach the limits of the instrument, or at least his own limits with it? Would everything become rote, a knotted snarl of reflexes? Just say "Bwire's last sonata" to him and, like the computer, he'd be programmed to perform it, down to the last nuance, all emotion canned, all spontaneity drained.

Did he indeed have the talent, the intelligence, the capability, to be anything other than a musician? He didn't care to be anything else now. But, in time, would he tire of the same old grind, over and over, repeated endlessly, until he'd lost count of the times, lost count, indeed, of the centuries? It seemed absurd and improbable, and yet . . . would the edge go out of his life?

Don't look a gift horse in the teeth, he told himself, not really understanding why anyone would want to look *any* animal in the teeth.

"Are you all right?" Pentland LaCroix's beautiful face hung over him.

"Yes, I'm fine. Just . . ."

"Drained?" He nodded. "I know what you mean. Sometimes I feel that way after a taping session."

He smiled in agreement but he wondered if it was the same. Could she ever really understand the solitude of the live performer? Her performance was distilled through many eyes and hands, those of the director and the technicians, repeated again and again until they had what they wanted. Although Garcia's performance could be enhanced or marred by the hands of technicians such as Steinbrunner, nothing could save him from his own mistakes and imperfections. He had one shot each night, and there were no retakes. Pentland LaCroix might be drained and exhausted at the end of a day's taping, but the emotional load that Garcia and Jorme went through was something she would never know.

"I brought you some champagne." He took the glass gratefully and drained half of it, barely tasting it. "That was easily the best concert that you and Jorme have given. I hope they taped it."

"They taped all of them."

"But they couldn't capture the feeling of being right here and seeing the music made right before your eyes."

"No. No, they couldn't."

"Sometimes," she said wistfully, "I wish I was in live theater. I envy you and Jorme so much, being able to put it all out on one line, one magnificent chance."

"You don't have any chances to correct mistakes." Garcia's voice was soft.

"No. You're naked out there. All on your own. It's all yours and no one can take that away from you."

"It can be frightening sometimes."

"Life always is. Or at least it should be. What's the sense in always doing the sensible thing, the safe thing? Sometimes I wish . . . sometimes I wish I were a musician rather than an actress."

Garcia took her hand. "Most musicians play in studios or at best in groups. There aren't many soloists who play live concerts any more."

"Maybe . . . maybe I could do something live, like those poets at The Welcome Machine. Do you think they'd be interested?"

"I'm sure they'd love to have you perform."

Her smile was cynical. "They'd love to have me perform naked."

Garcia raised his eyebrows. "You can't blame them for that, can you?"

She laughed, a full-throated laugh that yet was as dainty as crystal, and pulled her hand free. "Well, I see you've recovered from your depression. I think I'll go back to Jorme."

Garcia watched her sensuous departure, the graceful walk of an animal, tamed yet wild, civilized yet unspoiled.

Nearby, a young man sat in solitude, like Garcia, nursing his champagne. Garcia almost passed him by before he realized who it was.

"Philip! Come over here and talk to me."

The young man, who had a ragged rust-red beard and watery gray eyes, moved over. "You looked busy." His soft friendly voice betrayed nothing of the shyness that Garcia knew was there.

"You did a fine job tonight, Philip."

Philip shrugged. "It could've been better."

"You have nothing to be ashamed of."

Philip grinned suddenly. "Neither do you."

"What do you think of Jorme?"

"He's good, quite good. You'll have to watch out for him in a couple of years. He might take away your crown."

Garcia looked at his empty glass. "Sooner or later, someone's going to. It might as well be my own protégé. That would look a lot better."

There was a strange look in Philip's eyes as he regarded Garcia silently for a moment. "You're changing."

"Everyone changes."

"I'm glad. It's about time. First Stella Blue, and now Jorme."

And Shaara, Garcia thought, but he said nothing.

Philip closed the silence by asking about Bwire.

"He's dying, Philip; he's dying."

"I know. But is he dying well?"

Garcia looked at Philip, uncomprehending. "How can anyone die well?"

"Shakespeare said it once: 'Nothing became his life so well as the leaving of it.' Or something like that."

"But there's nothing I can do for him, Philip!"

"Sure there is. Just be there. Be his friend and his best student, as you've always been. That's all he asks; that's all he wants. Bwire's a good man, Garcia. He's very proud of you, and he has every reason to be." Philip got up. "Well,

I'd better be going. I've got to reset the lights for tomorrow night."

"You never stay at these things for very long."

"I'm not a very social person, I'm afraid. Parties get tedious and boring very rapidly."

"Philip." The technician looked at him, expectant. "Do you know if Elnor reviewed tonight's performance?"

Philip nodded. "I'm sure he did. He was on the net."

"Okay. Thank you."

Garcia watched Steinbrunner leave, feeling a little sorry for the technician, yet not a great deal, for Steinbrunner obviously didn't feel very sorry for himself. In fact, Garcia reflected, he seemed to feel a little sorry for Garcia . . . who had more than Steinbrunner would ever have.

There was a blare of noise and Garcia was jolted out of his reflections again, this time by the holovision that someone had turned on. The reception room had become a large life-size stage, and they were trying to find the critical reviews of the concert.

Jorme and Pentland came over to Garcia, the youngster's dirty blond hair seeming unruly and unkempt next to the HV star's brilliant dark waves. But anyone with half an eye could see how much the two of them were in love. Garcia envied them: what he shared with Shaara was a cold passion compared to what the two of them had. Slowly, other people drifted over to be near Garcia and Jorme: Justin Mead and his wife, dowdy but talented; Mars Ruby and a young man whom Garcia had heard referred to as an up-and-coming plastic artist; Renard, escorting a plain lady who was probably some producer's secretary. Suddenly, Garcia felt very lonely. He wished Shaara was out of the hospital and at his side.

The initial reviews all were very complimentary, picking on little details here and there, even on Steinbrunner's lighting at times. Some of them were embarrassingly gushy; even Jorme squirmed at the fulsome praise that was directed toward him.

Finally Elnor appeared on the stage. He was thin as a rail, almost to the point of emaciation, and he wore anachronistic spectacles that added to his scholarly air. Garcia had always wondered if they contained panes of ordinary glass.

"Ichabod Crane," someone muttered as Elnor peered out at his imaginary audience, as though he could actually see them. The critic was the master of the significant pause.

"Garcia and Jorme concluded their triumphant tour today with their second concert at the Radcliffe Memorial Auditorium. A full house of 402 was present in person, with a holovision audience rated at eight percent."

Elnor looked up from the sheaf of papers which he pretended to read and peered out at the viewers. "As I'm sure all of you know, Jorme is Garcia's first student and protégé. Before Garcia took him on as a pupil, Jorme had not given even a single solo concert, although he had been rated as one of the most promising students at the conservatory. Jorme has maintained his perfect record, since he has been sharing Garcia's concerts. It may be time that he went out on his own; it is not wise for Garcia to allow Jorme's mistakes to be forgotten in the wake of his own performances."

Elnor returned to his notes. "Jorme has improved immeasurably since his initial concert here at Radcliffe. The nervousness that was apparent that first night has disappeared from his performance. In its place, the emotion and fire of that performance have increased and are more in control. Nonetheless, the lack of precision and, in places, outright sloppiness . . ."

Garcia watched Jorme as Elnor savaged his performance. The jovial face took on a granitic stolidness, pain etched in the lines of his brow and around his eyes. Pentland, on the other hand, was a study of anger. She kept interrupting the holocast with exclamations of "That's not true!" and "He's crazy!" but Jorme stopped her simply by placing his hand on her shoulder.

Elnor then moved on to Garcia's own performance, which he praised quite openly while picking out every single failure of technique, no matter how minute, that Garcia himself had been aware of.

"It is to be hoped," Elnor concluded, "that Garcia's precision and technique will be mastered by his protégé, rather than Garcia being influenced by his student's sloppiness, which some critics have praised for its fire and energy. Several years ago Garcia seemed about to follow this path, but we can all be happy that he did not, and I hope he won't succumb to its wiles now.

"In sum, Garcia continues to move ever onward in the mastery of his subtle instrument, even though he is already far beyond any current practitioner of the art. His first student, Jorme, shows considerable promise and the restraining hand of his master may result in an autarist second only to Garcia."

The image faded, and the viewers began to stir, stretching their limbs and moving toward the hors d'oeuvres and drinks.

"Don't pay too much attention to Elnor," Garcia said to Jorme. "He doesn't understand anything except technique."

Jorme looked up at Garcia, trying to hide the hurt in his eyes. "I'll show him, Garcia. Don't worry. I'll show him."

CHAPTER 18

When Shaara finally agreed to see Garcia, she was sitting in an armchair in her hospital suite, wrapped in a light blue robe. When he moved to embrace her, she pushed him away.

"What . . . ?"

"Please, Garcia. There's still danger. My immune response hasn't fully recovered yet. Please. Sit down." She motioned to a seat on the far side of the room.

Garcia sat down slowly, looking at her. Her face was pale and she seemed somehow slighter, gaunt.

"Do I look that bad?" Her laughter was hollow.

"No, I just . . ."

She held up a hand. Garcia stopped, looking for the first time into her eyes, which seemed haunted with pain. "I know. I *do* look bad. Sometimes I think I'm not the same person." She looked away. "Father tried to warn me, but you won't know until you've been through it."

"Been through what?"

"The operation. The *second* operation. There's more to it than just implanting an artificial gland. The secretions of that gland, well, they have a very strong effect on the nervous system. It's been hell, Garcia, even with drugs. It's taken longer for my body to adapt to the new hormones than anyone else has so far."

"Is it worth it then?"

"Yes!" Her laugh was brittle. "Oh, God, Garcia, there were times in the past few weeks when I wished I was dead, when I begged them to kill me, do anything to stop the pain. There was nothing they could do. But now the worst of it is over, and my life means that much more to me. It's a very precious thing now, and those few days of pain are nothing compared to the centuries ahead." She leaned toward him then stopped herself. "And you too, Garcia. Please hurry. I've talked to Father and you can begin today. There's a limousine waiting for you outside and they'll take you to the laboratory. It'll only take a short time and then in a few months we'll be together for eternity."

"I don't know . . ." The pain and fear behind her eyes seared Garcia deeply.

"Please, Garcia. For me?"

"I . . ." What could he say? What could he do? "I'll think about it."

"Please, Garcia. Talk to Father."

On the journey to Muenstretiger's estate Garcia contemplated his course of action. The recognition of the pain that Shaara had gone through frightened him: he had never known much of physical pain himself and he feared it deeply. His missing arm began to twinge and ache as it hadn't in years. Was immortality worth such a price? Shaara had an answer for that: a few days of pain certainly were worth an eternity of life. He had no reply to that. He finally settled on an ambiguous solution: he would undergo today's operation, the brief excision of part of his thymus gland. By itself, it wasn't a final irrevocable decision for immortality. When the time came for the second operation, months from now, he could make his final decision.

Muenstretiger greeted him in the same brown study where they had first talked. "Shaara tells me you have some doubts about the operation."

"I've decided to go through with it. I thought it out on the way over."

"Good." Muenstretiger laid a hand on his shoulder with a gentle ease that was reassuring. "Dr. Gregg would be disappointed if he didn't have his promised victim today."

"But . . ."

Muenstretiger raised an eyebrow. "But what? What are your reservations, Garcia?"

"There's more to it than just a couple of operations, isn't there?"

"Of course. You're still not protected from diseases. All we've done is provide you with a system for replacing lost body cells, for maintaining youth, so to speak. What you do with that is up to you. You can sit back and grow fat, courting heart disease, or you can keep trim and fit."

"It just seems too easy, that this artificial gland would provide just the right balance of hormones or whatever."

Muenstretiger smiled. "Not really. The body has its own regulatory feedback systems, and this gland is fashioned from part of your own tissue, in fact, from one of the major regulatory organs. Of course, we have to keep close tabs on it, especially in the beginning, to make sure it doesn't run out of control."

"Has that happened?"

"A couple of times."

"What do you do then?"

Muenstretiger's smile was wan. "Remove the gland and start all over again."

Dr. Gregg had Garcia lie down on an operating table while a male nurse slapped an anesthetic patch on his neck. "You will truly be immortal now, Garcia."

What about you, Dr. Gregg? Garcia thought, and he was surprised when the doctor answered, "Me? Like most of those who developed this process, I too am immortal."

Of course. Garcia hadn't been aware that he had spoken and this time he managed to keep the thought to himself. One must have immortal technicians and scientists to guard the immortal wealthy and powerful and their immortal playthings. It made sense, it all . . .

. . . all what? Garcia tried to capture the thought, but it had already sprouted wings and flown away. He reached harder for it, but that only widened the distance between him and it, and he quit reaching, feeling a deep loss. Whatever the thought had been, it was a profound and important truth, and he feared having to relearn it again someday at a high cost.

"Ah, you are back with us, Garcia?" Dr. Gregg's voice, still sounding as though he was amused at some private joke, broke into Garcia's reverie. Garcia started to get up, but the doctor's hand on his right shoulder restrained him. "No, no. Not yet. Lie still for a few minutes yet. You'll be stiff for a little while. I made the incision through the left side of your neck. That way the muscles that control your right arm won't be affected."

"But . . ."

"Oh, I know. I'm not stupid. I know you need control of your left hand as well. Don't worry. You'll just be sore for a couple of days. You won't have lost any of your dexterity." The doctor released his grip on Garcia's shoulder. "You may sit up now if you want to."

Garcia did so. A knot of soreness sent spider tendrils of pain across his neck, through his shoulder, and up the back of his neck. He felt dizzy and weak.

"The chauffeur will take you back to your apartment." Garcia swung his legs over the edge of the operating table and sat there, head down, fighting the dizziness. "I couldn't help but spend a little time examining the work on your right shoulder. Excellent work, excellent. McLeod, of course, is a fine surgeon. You are very lucky."

"Yes. Yes, I am."

CHAPTER 19

Garcia wanted to take Jorme's mind off Elnor's criticism by suggesting that the two of them go to The Welcome Machine with Shaara and Pentland LaCroix. But Shaara wasn't willing to leave her father's estate. "Why don't you all just come over here instead?" she suggested.

"I was just thinking of a night out on the town for all of us, some excitement to keep Jorme busy. I thought maybe we could go to The Welcome Machine, like we did before."

"I can't do it, Garcia."

"Why not?"

"Things are different now."

"Different? Different how?"

"You know."

"No, I don't." Garcia struggled to get his voice back under control. "What are you talking about?"

"Can Jorme hear us?"

"No. He's in my workshop. He's a very understanding person, and he respects others' privacy."

"Okay. Garcia, try to look at it my way. I'm immortal now, and I just don't want to do anything that would endanger that."

"How is going out for a night on the town going to endanger your precious immortality?"

"I know it doesn't look that way to you, Garcia, from your viewpoint. It's rather limited, but you still don't see it."

"I don't think my viewpoint is limited."

"No, you wouldn't. I can understand that. After all, my own viewpoint was limited too, just a few short weeks ago. But things are different now. When you have your operation, then you'll understand. I think you probably already are beginning to understand. Think: why should I endanger centuries of life for just a few brief hours of enjoyment? Especially when the enjoyment can come here."

"Is that all I am to you? Enjoyment?"

"No, darling. Don't be a fool." Her voice was soft and consoling but the words bit deep into Garcia. "I don't have to go out into the city and endanger myself when you can come here where we'll both be safe from accidents and risk."

"That's not going to help Jorme any."

"All right, darling. You go out and have your fun tonight. But please take care of yourself and don't do anything rash."

Garcia watched in frustration as her image faded. Was she right? Would he feel the same way when he himself was immortal? Frightened to leave the safe warm confines of the Muenstretiger estate, where surely he would be living? Suddenly he didn't want to go out with Jorme and Pentland tonight—he remembered the crushing maw of a river cleaner closing on his arm years ago. Shaara was right —the world outside her safe little womb *was* dangerous. There were simple accidents and failures of equipment, and there was the ever present danger of other people's tempers. Even his own apartment, so dear and sacred to him, was more dangerous than Muenstretiger's estate.

"Well?"

"What?" Garcia looked up at Jorme. "Oh. No, she's still not completely recovered. We'll have to go alone. Why don't you call Pentland?"

"Do you think . . . I mean . . . I thought it was going to be the four of us, and . . ."

"I'll find someone." Garcia grinned. "I haven't erased my little black book yet."

He looked around the room while Jorme talked to Pentland. If he were to marry Shaara, he would have to give all this up and move onto her father's estate; that much was clear. She wouldn't come to live with him; she was rooted there and wouldn't leave for anything less than a national catastrophe. He touched the fireplace and its controls—on second thought, he probably wouldn't have to leave any of this behind. It could all be transported to the estate without leaving anything behind. He might even be able to have a genuine fireplace with a genuine wood fire in it . . . if Shaara didn't think it too dangerous.

"Pentland wants to talk to you." Garcia raised a questioning eyebrow but Jorme just spread his hands in a gesture of ignorance. Garcia walked over to the stage.

"Hi. What's the matter?"

"Jorme tells me Shaara isn't going with us."

"You know how it is. She's just had an operation and all . . ."

"Yes. What is this mysterious operation? You've never talked about it."

"No, I haven't." Garcia chuckled nervously. "You know

how I am. I really haven't the slightest idea what it was
about."

Pentland looked at him oddly. "If it was Jorme, I'd want
to know every detail I could."

"We're different people, Pentland."

She looked at him for a long moment. "Yes, we are."

Garcia looked at Jorme on the other side of the room,
engrossed in his autar. Jorme looked up suddenly, smiled,
then continued practicing. "Look, Pentland." Garcia's
voice was low and intense. "Shaara's okay. She's home
now. The important thing is to get Jorme to relax. He's
taking Elnor's criticism much too seriously. That's why I
wanted to go out tonight. You *will* go out with us to The
Welcome Machine, won't you?"

"Just you, me, and Jorme?"

"I'll find someone else. I'm not married to Shaara yet."

"Yet, huh? Okay. I'll be waiting for you."

CHAPTER 20

They passed through the maw of The Welcome Machine
and sat at one of the tables in the balcony, looking over its
edge at the students and others below. Another *grilly* band
was at work, this one without a distinguishing vocalist, and
the youngsters were busy writhing away their frustrations
on the dance floor.

"Why don't you and Pentland go down and dance?"
Garcia thought that the physical activity might help drain
away some of the youngster's tensions.

Pentland looked at Garcia. "I wouldn't dare."

"She'd be mobbed," Jorme said.

"I'm sorry. I wasn't thinking."

"I'll dance with you." Mars Ruby stood up. "Garcia
never dances, and I *love* to dance."

Jorme looked at Garcia, who nodded his approval.

Pentland waited until Jorme and Mars Ruby were gone,
then said, "She loves you, you know."

Garcia spread his hands in resignation. "Does she? I
don't know, Pentland. I know she cares for me more than
she cares for anyone else, but is that love?"

"If that isn't, what is?"

While Garcia pondered that, his thought processes
seeming to be incredibly slow, Pentland took his hand.
"You love Shaara, don't you?"

"I don't know. I guess so."

"You *guess* so. You're planning to marry her, aren't you?"

Stupefied, Garcia could only stare at her. Was he that transparent? "Do you women have some kind of a private hot line?" he asked at last.

Pentland laughed. "No. But you're not acting at all like the Garcia of old."

"You didn't *know* the Garcia of old."

"No, but I've heard enough about him. Anyway, even if I hadn't been able to guess, Mars Ruby would have told me." She looked down at the dance floor. "Look at them down there." Jorme and Mars Ruby were moving violently among the other violently-moving bodies, Mars Ruby's scarcely-covered breasts bobbing and jiggling. "I envy them in a way, you know?" She looked back at Garcia, who continued to stare at the dancers. "I wanted to be rich and famous, but I didn't realize how that restricted your movement and your freedom. I can't go down there and relax; I can't dance without worrying about someone coming up to me. I can't just go where the urge takes me. I have no control over my life. It's like being in prison."

"A pretty lush prison," Garcia said softly.

"Yes, but a prison nonetheless. You know a little of what I'm talking about, don't you?" Garcia nodded. "And it won't be long before Jorme will too." They were both silent a moment. "Is it true that you really don't dance, or do you just say that to keep from getting mobbed down there?"

"No, it's true." Garcia's voice was quiet and musing. "There never seemed to be enough time to learn."

"No. I guess not. There's never enough time. Sometimes I wish I could live forever."

"You could, you know."

"What?"

Garcia turned away, looking down at the dance floor again, surprised at himself, his guard down. "Nothing." But Pentland continued to stare at him, her countenance stern, her eyes searching.

"Garcia?" Her voice was soft. "Do you know something I don't?"

Well, why not? He had to tell *someone*. He couldn't keep it to himself forever. He turned back to her, back to those merciless eyes. "I said, you *could* live forever."

"That's what I thought you said."

"Listen, Pentland, if I tell you the whole thing, will you promise to tell no one else? Not even Jorme?"

She started to laugh, then stopped, realizing how serious Garcia was. "Why shouldn't I?"

"Not to protect me. To protect Jorme."

"Don't you think he's capable of protecting himself?"

"Look, you know how vulnerable he is. This would only make things worse for him."

Pentland looked at him for a moment longer, then glanced down at the table. "You might be right. Will you let me make the decision myself? You tell me what it is you have to tell me, and I'll decide whether or not Jorme should know."

It made sense to Garcia. In any case, the secret was out now, with a person who had not been selected yet for the immortals. Whether or not Pentland told Jorme, she would eventually tell someone else, and it would be over. What would he tell Jorme then? And Bwire?

Pentland listened quietly to Garcia's story, occasionally asking a question for clarification, until he had told her everything he could remember.

"And you've held this all inside you for months?" He nodded. "I don't envy you, Garcia."

"Will you tell Jorme?"

"No. You're right. Now's not the time for him to know. But I'll have to tell him eventually."

"What about anyone else?"

Her eyes were steel again. "No. I'll keep your precious little secret, Garcia."

"Don't be too hard on me."

"If I tell someone else, eventually Jorme will find out, and I don't want to do anything that will hurt him. But once he knows, the secret will be out, even if he says nothing."

Garcia nodded. "It's a frightening thought."

"You don't know how frightening. While you were gone, there were two riots down in the *barraque*. Once they get wind of this . . ." She stopped. There were no words to describe what would happen then, nor were any necessary.

"What are you two talking about?" Jorme entered the alcove and collapsed into his chair. His face was bright and shiny, and his breath came in heavy sighs. Mars Ruby's face was bright and shiny too, but she seemed in perfect control of her breath.

"I was telling him about the riots down in the *barraque* a couple of weeks ago. . . ."

CHAPTER 21

"Garcia. I have a call from Renard."

"Tell him I'll call him back. I'm busy right now." Garcia was halfway through a checkout of his autar, his special arm inserted deep into its innards, "seeing" the circuits with the aid of that arm's sensing devices, picking out needle points of dust and carefully removing them, checking capacitances and resistances, replacing parts and chips that seemed about to fail.

After a short pause the supervisor said, "He says it's important."

"Damn!" Garcia checked a molecular fusion he had made the last time on a chip that had had a microfracture. It still seemed secure, but he had his doubts. "Okay. I'll take it here."

"Garcia?" There was a strange edge to Renard's voice.

"I'm here."

"Turn on the holostage."

"I'm in my workshop." There was no stage in Garcia's workshop.

"Oh." Renard paused a moment. "Let me know when you've reached a breakpoint."

Garcia ran down the checklist in the repair arm's computer. He was slightly more than halfway done, but he could pick it up at any time in the future. "Go ahead."

"You're sure?"

"I'm sure. Go ahead." Garcia was getting annoyed. First Renard had interrupted him in the middle of working on his autar, and now he was wasting time.

"Uh, I don't know how to tell you this, Garcia, but . . . well, Bwire died thirty minutes ago."

Garcia stared at the autar in front of him, an uncomfortable warmth creeping up his chest. Although he wasn't crying, his eyes suddenly seemed hot. Even though he had been expecting it for such a long time, it still hurt. No more to know Bwire's exasperating peregrinations, to know his waspish tongue, to bask in the warmth of his rare praise. Somehow, he had never really believed that Bwire would die, that he would just slowly wither away as he had for the past few years, always there, always subtly guiding Garcia with his sarcasm. If it hadn't been for Bwire . . .

"Garcia?"

"Yes." Garcia cleared his throat. "I heard you, Renard. Thank you. Thank you very much."

"Is there anything I can do?"

"I don't know. I can't think of anything right now. I guess I'm not thinking too clearly."

"Well, don't worry about it. I'll take care of everything. I'll send the message and . . ."

"No!" Garcia's sharp response cut Renard off in mid-sentence. "I'll handle everything."

"Look, Garcia, there's no need to . . ."

"Renard," Garcia said softly, "Bwire was like a father to me. This is a private personal thing, okay?"

"Sure, Garcia. Sure."

Garcia sat in his workshop for a long moment, unseeing, his thoughts and emotions a chaotic jumble. Finally he asked the supervisor to connect him with Bwire's apartment, but the number had already been disconnected. While he tried to figure out what to do next, Jorme called. He already had the information that Garcia wanted.

"His daughter's going to take care of everything, Garcia. Did you know he had a daughter?"

"Yes." Bwire talked of her less and less as he had grown old. Garcia had met her only once. She must be nearly fifty now, Garcia thought, maybe older, but he didn't really know.

"I didn't. It's hard to think of Bwire having children."

Bwire had hundreds of children, Garcia thought, and he and Jorme were only two of them. But he was the favorite, he thought, jealously guarding that distinction.

"The cremation will be tomorrow."

So soon. So soon. Hardly cold and stiff, he would be reduced to elements and released. Would the soul fly upward and be consumed in the flames, never to know an immortality of any kind? The soul. Garcia had never known religion except at a distance, hearing of the dreams of immortality and a better life that waited after death for the workers in the *barraque*. He had never believed in the soul, in an afterlife, or in a reincarnation, but now he fervently wanted to believe, for Bwire if not for himself. It seemed unfair that so good a man as Bwire should just cease to be, without leaving anything behind but a few memories, traces of acetylcholine in a few brains that in their own time would cease to be as well, until the only thing that remained of Bwire would be a few words in a computer somewhere, a few on-and-off bits to be resurrected occasionally by some historian.

There had to be more. It just wasn't right; it wasn't fair. But who had ever told Garcia that the world was fair?

He contacted Bwire's daughter, who told him that Bwire had requested that he play a short Rujula requiem at the funeral. "You don't have to be here personally, of course. There's a holostage at the crematorium."

"I'll be there personally." He paused, uncertain how to mention this. "The last time I saw Bwire, he asked me to complete a composition for him."

"He left a number of things to you. Most of them are of no use to us, music and things like that."

And that was that. He would go to the funeral tomorrow, play the Rujula requiem for people who wouldn't appreciate it, for a man who would appreciate it but who wouldn't be able to hear it, who wouldn't be able to give him a critical appraisal when it was complete. It would be just an empty gesture for the empty husk of a man.

CHAPTER 22

Jorme and Pentland were already there when Garcia arrived for Bwire's funeral. Bwire's daughter and her children were also there along with several others whom Garcia didn't know, and a handful of Bwire's pupils and colleagues.

He went through the ordeal of greeting the family, forgetting names as quickly as they were mentioned, and went over to look at his mentor, lying in a stasis field on a block of plastigranite. Bwire was wearing his favorite blue robe, its folds neater and more orderly than ever they had appeared in life. The lines and creases of his face were relaxed and the hands that had become claws were at peace by his side. There was no hint of the sarcasm and the biting tongue, only a sad old man who had come to the end of his road.

"Garcia?" A small man with a fringe of red whiskers was at his side.

"Yes?"

The man introduced himself as a lawyer, the executor of Bwire's estate. He handed Garcia a large package. "He wanted you to have these. There's some personal things, and a note."

"Thank you."

"He also wanted you to have one of his autars."

"The best one," Bwire's daughter said in a bitter tone. "You'd think he would be more thoughtful of his family, wouldn't you, Garcia? I'm sure you understand . . ."

"Understand?"

"That autar is worth a great deal."

"I see." It seemed obscene to be talking like this in front of Bwire's corpse. Garcia's voice took on an edge of steel. "You want me to refuse my claim to the instrument."

"Well, it's the only honorable . . ."

"Bwire wanted me to have that instrument. He had his good and just reasons, I'm sure. You know very little about music, even though you're his daughter. That instrument, one of the finest in the world, could wind up in anybody's hands, if you were to have your way."

"Well, of course I'd be careful . . ."

"I *want* that instrument. In addition to its being so valuable, it meant a great deal personally to Bwire and hence to me as well."

The woman looked at Garcia angrily. "I thought you'd be more understanding than *that*." She started to turn away.

"I'll have it appraised and send you its value," Garcia said bitterly, his sorrow overwhelmed by the feeling of being soiled by this contact with Bwire's daughter. He turned to the lawyer. "You'll have it sent to me?"

"Of course."

Sullenly he played the Rujula requiem, trying to lose himself in the music and his last homage to Bwire, but the day now had a bitter taste to it. He left as soon as he was done, the tension in his wake being swept up by the good-natured Jorme and the levelheaded Pentland.

"What did Bwire leave you?" Jorme asked. "In the envelope."

"Just some papers. He wanted me to finish one of his compositions."

"That's great! You'd be an incredible composer."

Garcia looked at his pupil. "Just because I've mastered one instrument doesn't mean I can compose music. It's something else entirely."

"But surely the two skills would complement each other?" Pentland said.

"If you've got both of them. I don't."

"Are you sure?"

Garcia grunted. "I took a composing class at the conservatory. I didn't do very well in it. Bwire knew it."

They went to Garcia's apartment, where Garcia poured some wine and put on a holocube of one of Bwire's performances, when he was still young, younger than Garcia was now.

The lines of old age were gone. One could not even guess where they might appear on that sharply handsome face with the straight nose that would turn into a parody of a cruel beak with age. The gray and brittle hair was dark and sleek, full of body. The eyes that were so piercing and the smile that was so full of bite were now gentle and misted, no trace of sarcasm present. And the hands . . . the gnarled and twisted claws were supple and moved with a life of their own across the strings of the instrument, darting rapidly to the controls to change the program as the flow of the music altered. Bwire had never mastered control of his little finger the way Garcia had, needing the strength of two fingers to change the settings, but at his best, when this tape had been recorded, Bwire had a speed that Garcia had never quite matched.

"He was . . . good, wasn't he?" Pentland's voice was oddly choked. Garcia wondered whether she was somehow touched by Bwire's death, through him and Jorme, or by the music that they were listening to. He was pleased that she didn't say great or some other superfluous word. "Good" was an understatement, but it fit Bwire more elegantly than some more grandiose word.

"He was very good," Garcia said quietly.

"I've seen some of his cubes, but I don't think I've ever seen this one."

"It's a private recording. There aren't many copies of it around."

There was a scattering of applause; it had been a very small and select audience. Bwire looked out of the holostage directly at Garcia, a strange saintly smile on his face, and Garcia felt tears come to his eyes. Then the master looked down at his instrument, the very instrument that now belonged to Garcia, and began playing again.

Garcia opened the packet on his lap. As he had expected, there were quite a few sheets of music, annotated in Bwire's careful spidery hand. On top was a short note, written in that same spidery script, shaky yet firm:

Garcia—When you read this, I shall be dead, probably by several days. It doesn't matter. I've led a good and enjoyable life, even exciting at times, and the best parts are over. I am not "going gentle into that good night," as the phrase has it—I intend to give Old Man Death a good thrashing when I meet him. Garcia smiled. *You were the best of my pupils, not despite your recalcitrance and stubbornness, but because of it. I learned more from you than from all the rest of my students put together. It is one reason why I suggested you take a student: I suspect one learns more from teaching than from being taught.*

You have always placed too much emphasis on your playing. It has become your entire life, and that has placed restrictions on you which you do not even suspect. I cried for you and with you over the death of Stella Blue, but I was at the same time glad for you, because it was a step forward, out of your shell.

Now it is time for the next step. I wish I could be here to share it with you, but perhaps it is my own death that will instigate your taking it. Perhaps not. Perhaps I put too much emphasis on my own influence on you.

"No," Garcia said softly, almost choking on the syllable. Jorme looked over at him with a questioning look on his face, and Pentland laid a cool hand on his.

"You loved him, didn't you?"

Garcia nodded, unwilling to trust his voice, and continued reading.

There is something growing inside you, a restlessness. I don't know its exact cause, but please don't disregard it. Follow it, Garcia. It may be hard at times, but you will not regret it. Reach, strive. Go over the edge.

Good luck, my friend and my finest pupil. I have faith in you.

Garcia looked up from the note, only barely aware of Jorme and Pentland, seeing only that falsely substantial image of a man he barely remembered, young and full of life, playing his autar as though his life depended on it.

CHAPTER 23

The holostage was silent; Bwire was back in his cube. The false logs in Garcia's fireplace popped and crackled. The three of them were slightly tipsy from the wine; Garcia knew they would all feel its effects the next morning.

"Did you know those other people at the funeral?" Pentland asked.

"Yes. Some of them." Garcia's voice was soft. "There were several people there from the conservatory, students of Bwire's, some of my classmates."

"You hardly talked to them."

"No. We weren't friends. I didn't have many friends back then."

Pentland touched him on the arm. "You've got friends now."

"Yes. I guess I have."

Jorme wandered around the room, half drunk, looking at the false books in the bookcases, peering into gargoyled corners, staring at the pseudo-leather furniture. For a time he had toyed with his autar, playing aimless random tunes —even drunk, he was too good a musician to play something with no musical value. Now he stood in front of one of the pseudo-bookcases, his fingers probing its side.

"Hey, Garcia, something's wrong here. I think your bookcase is falling apart."

"No. That's the emergency exit."

"Emergency exit?"

"In case of power failure or something like that, and the elevators quit working, that kind of thing."

"No kidding? How does it work?"

"You have to operate it manually." Garcia walked over to the fireplace. A small lever disguised as a poker came down slowly and the bookcase swiveled to reveal an unadorned and functional door behind it.

"Where does it lead?"

"To a stairway."

Jorme opened the door and walked out onto a naked cement landing. The stark functional unfinished quality of the emergency exit contrasted sharply with the opulence of Garcia's apartment. The cement was rough to the touch, feeling almost as though it could break the skin at the tips of one's fingers as Jorme ran his over it. Stairways led from the platform, one up and one down.

"That one goes all the way down to the ground floor?"

Garcia nodded. "I have no desire to follow it, however, unless it becomes absolutely necessary."

"And that one?" Jorme pointed to the stairway going up.

"To the apartments above mine, I would suppose."

"And the roof?"

"Perhaps."

Jorme started up the stairway. "Let's find out. You're not far from the top, are you?"

Garcia shook his head. "Not so fast. What do you want to go up there for? You won't see anything you can't see from my workshop."

"Come on, Garcia. Just for the hell of it. What do you say? Pentland?"

The actress looked at Garcia hopelessly. Well, why not? Perhaps this was what Bwire had in mind. The youthfulness and the playfulness of Jorme, his boyishness, was something that Garcia had never known. He had always been a serious, solitary youth, a bit afraid of other children, unable to join in their play. It seemed to come naturally to other people, to Jorme, to Justin, to Mars Ruby, even to Pentland and Shaara; but Garcia had to work at it and learn it.

"Okay. Let's go."

Four flights later, the stairway ended at a doorway. Jorme tried the door but it wouldn't open.

"It's probably the top apartment, and it certainly wouldn't open for us," Garcia said.

"You try."

Garcia tried to open the door but had no better success than Jorme had had.

"There's a lock over here." Pentland pointed to the small space on the door frame. "Why don't you try that?"

Garcia pressed his thumb against the space and the door swung openly smoothly, letting in a small cool evening breeze and the faint scent of smoke and oil, and whispers of distant sounds. Hesitantly, they entered a small dusty room at the top of the building. It was filled with machinery. Even as they stood there, the machinery began to whine. "That must be the elevator," Jorme said.

Garcia wanted to get as far away from it as possible, his heart suddenly pumping wildly as he thought of how many times he had trusted his body and his life to that fragile, whining piece of machinery. Machines died too, just like men, and they often took men with them when they died.

"Look!" Pentland had wiped away a clear space on one of the dusty windows in the shed. "It's beautiful!"

Through the small clear space they could see the lights of the city spread out before them, as they could be seen from Garcia's workroom. The young lovers pressed against the glass, looking out.

"Don't you want to see, Garcia?"

"I can see just as good a view from the comfort of my workroom."

Jorme was prowling around again, and suddenly he opened a door that Garcia hadn't been aware of, letting the breeze that had circulated softly in the shed become a blast of spring wind that lifted dust and scattered papers and spread them randomly throughout the tiny building. The small building was suddenly full of sound, the wind like a synthesizer, the underlying sounds of the city running a faint counterpoint.

"My God!" The awe in Jorme's voice brought Garcia reluctantly over to his side, where Pentland had already rushed when Jorme had opened the door.

The city now was clearly visible all around them, a panoramic view that dwarfed the limited one from Garcia's workshop. All the strings of light seemed to converge on this building, like spokes in a wheel, although Garcia knew that it was only an illusion, like the illusion that the Earth was the center of the universe. Across the spokes, other rays of light crossed and recrossed, moving out in waves of light from the building to the distant horizon, until they disappeared in the distance. The jewels of the city glowed and glittered all around them. The wind blew viciously across the top of the building, carrying traces of smoke and remnants of odd perfumes, intermingled smells of distant factories and nearby buildings. Although the top of the building had been swept clean by the wind, the dust and rubbish inside the small structure at the top of the elevator shaft was now available for the wind to play with, and it swirled and mixed around the little construction gleefully, moving dust out into the night air and blowing papers into the far distance.

"It's beautiful!" Pentland moved out onto the roof of the building.

"Be careful." Garcia was fearful of going out any further on the roof than the safe confines of the doorway.

"Don't worry."

"Is the view from your workshop as good as this?" Jorme asked.

"No. But it's safer." And the roar of the city was unheard there, its rhythms like a fast-beating heart unfelt.

"What's that?" Pentland pointed to an actinic glare that pierced the sky's darkness to the south, some distance away.

"That must be one of the shuttles going up to the starship," Jorme said. "The launching ground is down there on the peninsula."

The two lovers walked out onto the roof, moving fearlessly closer to the edge, while Garcia stayed near the elevator housing, fear molten inside his chest. He became more acutely aware of the steady hum and rhythm underneath the singing of the wind. The wind's voice rose and fell, sometimes so loud it seemed to contain all the sounds of the world, then falling to a faint susurrus under which the steady hum and rhythm of the city could be heard, the distant call of a muted foghorn or other warning device, the faint grinding of the river cleaners.

"Don't go too near the edge," he shouted out. "Be careful! This wind could blow you right off."

"Don't worry." Pentland's voice was almost carried away by the wind. Her dark hair blew wildly in the wind, visible only by the flickering glitter of light that it reflected in prismatic shards.

When they finally returned to the shed, her face was alive and aglow, as was Jorme's. The effect of the beauty of the scene, of the wind, made them more alive and fresh and vibrant than Garcia himself had ever felt, more so perhaps than he had ever seen anyone look before.

CHAPTER 24

Garcia stared at the notes in front of him, but he didn't really see them. His mind wandered as he tried to follow Bwire's music, but he wasn't yet aware that his concentration was gone. Looking at the key change in the middle of the second movement, he had begun daydreaming about the possibility of keying in a fret change at that point, so that the new key would use natural harmonies rather than the tempered scale. The problem with keying in the change was that the performer would then be unable to perform while the change was taking place. To rely on the computer to maintain the melodic flow was repugnant to Garcia. However, if there were some way to maintain a balance during the key change, sliding with the flow . . .

He had spent fifteen minutes playing with key changes on the autar, trying to find ways to maintain melodic flow during the change, but not succeeding. The computer was too fast for him, and his pressure on the keyboard during the change modified the speed of the key change in an unpredictable manner.

While the tension of the strings could be varied one by one through programming, it was not possible to change the fret pattern except across the whole keyboard. Still, there was no reason why it had to be that way. It was just that no one had ever thought of changing one fret at a time before. He would call Althor Burn to see if a special autar could be made that would allow modular changes to the fret pattern. And while he was at it, why not allow the speed of the changes to be determined by the performer instead of always at a fixed speed?

He looked at the music, seeing it again for the first time in minutes. There was no sense in working further on the concerto until he had talked to Althor Burn, indeed, not until he had such an autar in his hands. That would take months.

Months. Months from now, he would be immortal. Then would it matter? Yes, he knew it would. He would no longer be thinking in terms of leaving behind something besides a few ephemeral cubed performances. What did it matter what modifications and improvements he made to the instrument? What did it matter whether or not he left behind his own concertos and compositions? After a couple of hundred years, much less a thousand, would it matter to him?

As if in answer to his thoughts, Shaara chose this moment to call him. "Why don't you move here so we can be together again?" she suggested. "I haven't seen you in so long . . ."

"I will. Don't worry. But I can't leave here just yet."

"Why not? We can reconstruct your apartment without any trouble. I worry about you, Garcia. So much could happen to you. It would be such a tragedy if something were to happen to you when you were so close to immortality."

"Don't worry. I can take care of myself. And it's not nearly as dangerous out here as you think."

"That's what you say now. When you're immortal, you'll realize how precious your life is and how foolish it is to endanger it in silly ways. . . ."

As she talked, Garcia thought about the night before, when he had stood on the roof with Pentland and Jorme. They had not been afraid of going out on the roof, exposing themselves to the wind and to danger, however slight, while he had cowered against the elevator housing. They had been so alive when they had returned, while he had felt half-dead with fear. If he had not had immortality dangling in front of him like a carrot, would he have joined them? Would he have known their exhilaration, the sharp knife-edge of daring the inevitable, of spitting in the face of the grave?

"Darling?"

"I'm sorry. What did you say?"

"Father's giving a small party tomorrow night. All the immortals will be there, and we'd like you to come."

"Of course."

"The way things are going, it may be the last time all the immortals will be able to gather together in one place."

"How's that?"

"There'll be too many of us soon. Besides, it wouldn't be a good idea for all of us to gather at one time. We'd all be too vulnerable. It would be more than a tragedy, it would be a disaster, if all the immortals were destroyed."

"Yes, I suppose it would be."

"So I'll see you tomorrow night?"

"Of course."

"I can hardly wait, Garcia."

"Neither can I." Why then did he feel so reluctant, why did the prospect seem a dreary one?

"And please think about moving out here as soon as possible."

He looked again at Bwire's half-finished composition. Would any of the people at the party understand anything about it?

CHAPTER 25

One of Muenstretiger's chauffeurs picked Garcia up and drove him through the streets in a car that seemed more armored tank than limousine. Most of the same people were there who had been at the previous party, but Jack Orion notably was absent. Shaara's "small party" included close to one hundred people.

Garcia realized that, although his own name and face were better known and more easily recognized than any of the other immortals and immortals-to-be, it was they who really controlled things. He was just a pawn, the court jester to Muenstretiger's court, his captured pet monkey, a prize to display as he would a painting by an old master or a sculpture or a rare recording or a fine wine.

"Are all the people here immortal?" he asked Shaara.

"Most of them. Some of them have yet to take the treatment, and others, like my father, are already too old for it. But their sons and daughters have or will."

"Where's Dr. Gregg?"

"This is a party for just the immortals."

"But hasn't he taken the operation?"

"It's not the same thing. They are"—she paused, searching for the appropriate word—"technicians. They wouldn't be interested in people like us."

Garcia remembered their first meeting, when she had described herself apologetically as a social butterfly. Now she seemed to revel in her position; she was in her element, and he was a fish out of water.

Mont'Illiano placed a friendly hand on Garcia's shoulder. "It's good to see you again. A shame you didn't bring your autar. I understand you're going to join us."

"I'm thinking about it, yes," Garcia said slowly.

"Good! We need someone here besides all these old stodgy people without any talent except for making money."

"Monty!" Shaara admonished him.

"Well, it's true. That's all I do: just charm money out of our stockholders." He turned back to Garcia. "I understand one of your teachers died recently, ah . . ."

"Bwire."

"Yes. He supposedly was the finest autarist of his day."

"I learned a great deal from him."

"All the more reason why you should complete your treatment as soon as possible. Artists like you are rare; you're national treasures and should be treated as such."

"Put in dusty cabinets and taken out on holidays?" Garcia had tried to make the tone of his voice light, but there was a trace of bitterness there nonetheless.

Mont'Illiano looked at him sharply. "No, that's not what I meant. But it *is* true that you'd have to curtail your performance schedule drastically. It's one thing for an ephemeral person to do as much as he can in the short time he's allowed, but now we're freed from those restrictions, and we must take the long view."

"I'm afraid I haven't gotten used to thinking in those terms."

"None of us have yet. We're still learning. But we can afford to go cautiously, one step at a time."

And what would that mean for the electromotive industry, the communications industry, the pharmaceutical industry? A slow appraisal, perhaps centuries in length, of any developments. With the emphasis on those developments that would benefit the immortals. Such as a rejuvenation for those who had been in their late years when the discovery was made. Garcia felt as if he were on the edge of an important revelation, but he had no idea yet what it might be.

"Have you met President Quan?" Mont'Illiano asked, introducing Garcia to a small man with a nervous energy that seemed out of place among these serene captains and ladies of industry.

"I believe we are the only non-immortals here," he said to Garcia.

"What about the servants?"

"Oh yes. I forgot about them."

"Do they know about the process?"

"Oh no. I'm sure that Muenstretiger hasn't informed them about it. After all, we have to inform the public about this very quietly. There isn't enough expertise and equipment yet to offer immediately to any but a small portion of the people. You can imagine the consequences if the information were to leak out to the public."

Garcia could and he wondered how much longer the secret could be kept. The people at this "small party" talked openly and freely to each other about their status, ignoring the servants as though they weren't even there. If they hadn't known about the immortality process before this evening, surely some of them knew about it now. Some would keep their own counsel, perhaps offering their silence to Muenstretiger in return for the operation, but not all of them.

"Are you planning on another trip to The Welcome Machine afterwards?" he asked Mont'Illiano.

"Oh no." Mont'Illiano's laughter seemed hollow. "Things are different now, you know. I have to take care of myself now. You understand, don't you?"

Garcia nodded, thinking that maybe he understood more than Mont'Illiano himself did.

CHAPTER 26

"Garcia, I want to talk to you." There was an edge to Jack Orion's words and an intensity to his expression that Garcia had never seen before.

"Go ahead. Talk."

"I don't know if I should over this line. Maybe I should come over in person."

"Orion, I'm a busy man. Tell me what it is you want or don't bother."

Orion hesitated, his face a mask of indecision. "All right. Listen, are you still seeing Shaara Muenstretiger?"

"What do your spies tell you?"

"Cut it out, Garcia." Orion was exasperated and Garcia realized he was on the edge of losing control. His face was haggard, and its lines and wrinkles were emphasized by his weariness. "We're both on the same side."

"All right, all right. Yes, I'm still seeing her. If you must know, we're thinking of getting married." There. It was out, a bit to Garcia's own surprise.

But not to Orion's. "I was afraid of that," he said wearily. "Listen, I've found out what I was looking for, and I think you should know too, just . . . just in case."

"Just in case of what?"

"Never mind." Orion took a deep breath and the old confidence and brashness returned. "I've been hearing lots of ugly rumors lately, and I'm pretty sure they're true. I've tracked them down, and I trust my informants. It all holds together." Garcia waited. "Muenstretiger has discovered a way to make people immortal and he and the rest of the rich people are now immortal, including Shaara."

"That's absurd." Even if Jack Orion's facts were slightly askew, the basic fact was true. But Garcia would never admit it to Orion.

Orion peered at Garcia, trying to pierce his bluff. "You don't know anything about this?"

"How could I?"

"How could you? You're thinking of marrying Shaara, you've been to several of their parties, one where immortality was mentioned openly among the guests. Garcia, how could you *not* know?"

Garcia let out a weary breath. "Orion, you've had more to do with these people than I have, and how long has it taken you to find this out? I'm just a toy to them, a musician, an entertainer."

Orion sat back, obviously wanting to believe Garcia but still uncertain. "In any case, the news is out, and I'm going to blow it sky high this evening. There's nothing they can do to stop me. But I'm disappointed in you, Garcia; I had hoped for better things from you."

"I'm sorry. I don't live my life for your approval, Orion. I'm a musician, a performer, and that's what my life revolves around. Everything else is secondary."

"There are more important things to life than music."

"So they tell me." Garcia made no attempt to keep the sarcastic edge out of his voice.

Jack Orion sat on the holostage, his head nodding slowly as he looked at Garcia. "Some day, Garcia, some day . . ." And he broke the connection.

Garcia sat there, still watching the stage as though Orion were still on it. So the commentator finally knew. It wasn't surprising; the surprising part was that it had taken him so long to find out. Immortality wasn't something you could keep a secret for very long. And now what would happen? Orion would tape his commentary immediately and in a very short time the world would know, high and low, small and great. And Garcia would have to face his friends and tell them that he was one of the elect and they were not.

"Supervisor. Get me Mont'Illiano's office at Metropolitan."

A few seconds later a strange slender young man appeared on Garcia's holostage. "Can I help you?"

"I'd like to talk to Mont'Illiano."

"He's busy right now. I can take a message for him."

"I need to talk to him right now. This is important."

"I'm sorry. I can't do that. If you'll leave a message, he will call you right back."

Angrily, Garcia broke the connection. One of *them?* No, he wasn't part of Mont'Illiano's society, any more than he was part of Jack Orion's imaginary romantically-tinged *barraquistes*. He was himself, Garcia, and no one else. If he belonged to any group, it was that of musicians, but he could only call a handful of them his friends—Bwire, Jorme, Justin Mead. Who else? Who else, indeed?

Should he call Shaara? No, leave her out of this, leave them all out of it. But he was alone—he needed the advice of Bwire, but that advice was forever beyond him. He paced the apartment, solitude bearing on him like the merciless rhythm of *Bolero*. Perhaps . . . perhaps . . .

"Supe, try to get Jorme for me."

But when Jorme appeared on his holostage, Garcia didn't know what to say, how to tell Jorme what he wanted and needed. "Are you busy tonight?" he asked at last. "I'd like to just go out for a couple of hours." Jorme was hesitant. "What's the matter? Did you and Pentland have something planned for tonight?"

"No. No. She's over at Metropolitan tonight, working. But . . . I'm afraid I don't understand, Garcia. I mean, what did you want to do?"

Garcia smiled, realizing how out of character it was for him to suggest a night out on the town. "I'm not sure I can explain it, Jorme. I just need to get out of here and do something with some friends, and I thought of you and Justin. Do you mind?"

"No. Sure. Of course not."

Justin was delighted with the idea, and they met him at The Welcome Machine shortly after dusk. It was too early for any of the real action; it was strictly *ordinary* time, music to fill the souls and titillate the minds of young straights and newcomers looking for the heart of the city. The real grotesquerie would not begin for hours. Jorme didn't seem to mind, but Justin was restless.

"Let's go down to the *barraque*."

"I don't know." Garcia was hesitant, a bit fearful and uncertain.

"Look. This may be your last night out on the town before you get married. Then that'll be the end of that. You don't know what it's like."

Garcia smiled. "Yes. I've noticed how you never get out at all these days."

Justin laughed. "Touché." He held his hands up in a gesture of defeat. "But it will be awhile before the novelty wears off. What about it, Jorme? Want to go down to the *barraque?*" Jorme shrugged his shoulders. "We can go down and see Garcia's old haunts. What was the name of that place where you met Stella Blue?"

"The Row Jimmy."

"Right. Come on. We can come back here later."

The electrocab left them off at street level, several levels above the *barraque*, and they descended by the old stone wall, down one of the few lighted stairways remaining, to the noise and commotion of the *barraque* night.

Although the *barraque* had many old street lights, most of them were shattered and broken, and the three musicians walked in shadow. A riverfront portion of town, it had known its ups and downs, prosperity, decay, the rise back to being an attraction where craft shops and expensive restaurants were found, another decay, a time of expensive gambling casinos that naturally ran down to vice and corruption, and so on, swinging back and forth. Now it was on the rise again: in a few years it would probably be the chic spot in which to live and carouse. Right now, however, figures moved through the shadows, some stumbling and reeling. From the bars and clubs, the music was often drowned out by laughter and loud conversation, sometimes by angry shouts and cries.

Most of the buildings were constructed of centuries-old brick, the crumbling mortar patched and shored dozens of times in thousands of places. The pavement of the streets was cracked and holed, pitted and scarred.

If there were few street lights to provide illumination, there was some light that streamed out of the establishments, although many kept a dim glow for atmosphere and for illegal transactions.

The Row Jimmy was gone. Its windows were broken and there were a couple of rotting boards hammered across its closed door, as if to stop anyone who didn't want to enter through the windows. Inside was darkness—the place might be empty or it might harbor a dozen thugs; it was impossible to tell.

"The famous Row Jimmy," Garcia said sardonically. "Can I buy you boys a drink?"

"No respect for history," Justin said.

They walked slowly down the cracked street. In other bars, heavy-set men in grimy clothes talked and drank. Nearly every bar had a stopgo table, some of them broken. Nearly every third bar had a *grilly* band, some worse, some better, than the one Garcia had heard at The Welcome Machine.

They chose a bar that was quieter than the others. The twenty or so people in it morosely and bitterly nursed their drinks. The bandstand in the far corner apparently had not been used in quite some time: its stage was littered with plaster, dust, and trash. The two chairs on it were broken and mangled; the microphone stand that rose from the base was without a microphone.

"Welcome to the *barraque*," Garcia said to Jorme as

they sat down at a table chosen at random from the many empty tables in the bar.

"I'll get our drinks." Justin headed over to the bar.

"I've *been* to the *barraque* before many times." Jorme's voice indicated the insult he felt at the patronizing tone of Garcia's. "I know what it's like."   .

"Probably better than I do."

"Perhaps."

Justin returned with their drinks. "I'm not sure it was a good idea to choose this place," he said. "After all, there must be some reason why there's so few customers here while there's so many in the other bars."

Garcia tasted his drink. "What does it matter?"

"Maybe it's because nothing's happening here," Jorme said. "Everyone's going to the bars where something's happening."

"Great!" Justin stared at them. "We go out for a night on the town and pick the bar where nothing's happening."

"Garcia," a guttural voice said as a heavy hand fell on Garcia's shoulder. He turned around to see Auguste, the gorilla who had been working at the Row Jimmy when Garcia had first met Stella Blue. "You play?" Auguste gestured toward the dusty bandstand.

"I can't. I don't have my autar with me. You work here now, Augie?"

"Yuh. Come?" Augie started toward a door at the back of the bar, and Garcia got up to follow him.

"Where are you going?" Jorme asked.

"Don't worry. Augie's okay. He used to take care of me back when I hung around here years ago."

In the dingy stockroom, piled high with cases of liquor

and other supplies, Augie led Garcia to a battered old guitar, half of its strings gone, and the others too stiff with time to play. "You play?" Augie repeated.

"I can't play this, Augie. The strings are no good."

"I fix maybe. You wait."

While waiting for the gorilla to return, Garcia looked around the storeroom. Small animals rustled in the dark back corners, and something chittered overhead. He felt shivers go up his spine as he thought of someone spending his entire life in a place like this. Who would want to be immortal then?

Augie returned with the bar's owner, a small man with a lined face, looking every bit the hustler he was. "Garcia? Are you really Garcia? Augie says you want to play."

"No. *Augie* wants me to play. But I can't play this." Garcia held up the guitar.

"But you *will* play?" the owner asked eagerly. "I have strings for it."

Garcia shrugged. "Sure. Why not?"

The owner hesitated a moment, then said, "I have an autar, too, if you'd like to play that instead. It's not a very good one, of course, but . . ."

"Let me see it."

When the owner hurried off to fetch his autar and the guitar strings, Garcia went back to the table with the battered guitar.

"What the hell is *that*?" Jorme asked.

"A guitar. What does it look like?"

"I don't know. Don't tell me you're going to try to play it."

"I might." Garcia began stripping off the remaining

strings. A couple of the other customers looked over in lackadaisical interest. He wiped off the plaster and dust that covered its surface. The guitar was not a good one—its plastic body was cracked in several places, and the neck was beginning to separate from the body. Still, it looked playable.

The owner returned with the strings and his autar. He was right—it was one of the cheapest autars around, with barely a 12K memory. It was autars like this that made amateurs give up. Even when Garcia keyed the tuning button, the autar still wasn't in tune. He had to tune it manually, not an easy job on an instrument that wasn't meant for manual tuning.

"Think you can play this thing?" he asked Jorme.

The youngster looked at it doubtfully. "I suppose so. But I don't know if I want to."

"Did you bring your flute with you?" he asked Justin.

"Of course." Justin took the flute out of his jacket pocket and began assembling it, while Jorme played the autar softly and Garcia began restringing the guitar. Augie stood over them, watching eagerly.

"You play now?" he asked when Garcia had finished restringing the guitar.

"We'll try."

"Wait." The gorilla went into the back room again, returning with a broom. He swept off the stage, threw the broken chairs off it, and picked up three new ones from the tables. He looked ruefully at the empty microphone stand. "Do you need?" he asked as the three musicians came up to the stage.

"No. That's all right, Augie. We don't need it."

Augie smiled one of his rare smiles. "You like?"

"It's great, Augie." He patted the gorilla on the back. "Everything's fine."

"Augie fix good."

"Some night on the town," Justin said.

"How are you at *grilly?*" Garcia asked Jorme.

"Not much better than those guys at The Welcome Machine. I used to listen to it a lot, but I never played much of it."

"No time like the present to learn. You'll have to lead. I don't think you could do much following with that instrument."

They started off with some soft classical music, easily accessible to the *barraquistes*, with a steady rhythm from the autar, Garcia and Justin running harmonies around Jorme's melodic line. Several times he and Justin clashed, sometimes they chose the same harmony line, but no one else in the bar was aware of it.

As they played, Garcia became aware of the audience in the bar muttering his name over and over again: "Garcia!" "What's he doing here?" "That's his student. What's his name?" And the name of Stella Blue also surfaced and then went down, coming up again. It was a strange bifurcation of his energies and concentration, that was present in his usual concerts but was enhanced in this small bar until it reached a peak he hadn't known since his brief span as a guitarist at the Row Jimmy: he was two people, at once aware of the audience and their reaction to his music, and at the same time caught up in the music itself and pushing it to its limits. The two streams augmented each other—as the audience reacted to the music, Garcia became more involved with it, and their reaction became stronger.

It was no longer three musicians trying to find one another. He had played often enough with Jorme and Justin separately to understand them and to have a good idea where each of them would go next in their melodic structures. Justin and Jorme still had to learn to work with each other, but they were professionals enough to do it well, if unspectacularly. A few words were all that was necessary: "Radcliffe's *Goldfinch*" from Garcia, and Jorme slowed down the tempo as Garcia made the change from the simple exercises to the brief sonata; "Plastic Mother," Justin said (unexpected from him since he wasn't a *grilly* enthusiast), and Garcia strummed rhythm as the flute player went into the stratosphere; "Norwegian Wood" from Jorme, and he took the lead on the old folk tune.

Outside in the *barraque*, the wave of information went out like the ripples from a rock thrown in the river: "Garcia's back!" "He's at Wood's Hole." The quiet bar became jammed, people shouting their favorite songs, screaming. A woman, her face horribly disfigured, moved to the front of the crowd as Justin, Jorme, and Garcia started to play "Concrete Lover." She began singing, in a clear liquid voice that contained all the pain and ache of the *barraque*:

> "Concrete lover, hard as a rock,
> Brittle as ice, a key with no lock."

As she moved toward the stage, Augie moved to block her from the platform. Garcia gestured him away and she moved up to the stage, warbling liquid sighs when there

were no words, weaving connections among the three musicians, dropping almost into a tenor at times. Garcia looked
at Justin, who smiled back; Jorme was too busy with the
unfamiliar autar, his brow furrowed in concentration as he
tried to keep up with the veteran musicians, sweat dripping
down his cheeks. The woman moved over to him and
mopped his face, then did the same for Justin and Garcia.

Finally they stopped, and the owner brought them great
mugs of beer. Garcia had never cared much for the drink,
but right now anything cold felt good.

"What's your name?" he asked the woman.

"A name. What does it matter?" She touched her face.
"They call me Parrakeet or Warbler or Thrush or Canary.
It changes but the meaning's always the same. Will you
play some more?"

Garcia nodded. "You will sing?" She nodded back.

More mugs of beer joined the empty ones on stage and
suddenly there was money, the paper of the *barraque*,
coins, thrust at them. Justin picked it up and gave it to the
girl: "Take it. We don't need it." She hesitated, then
scooped up the money.

Garcia looked at Jorme, who was grinning dazedly.
"How did you like that?"

"It was more fun than the concerts."

Garcia nodded. It was. There had been an immediacy to
their playing that had never been present during a concert. The playing had been ragged and frequently out-of
tune, since neither he nor Jorme was familar with the instruments they were playing, and the three of them had
never played together before. It all had to come out from
inside them—they couldn't rely on technique and ability

only. If he could just get this spirit during a performance or a recording . . . but it was gone, only a memory now, and it would have to be recaptured again and again. It could never be recreated or relived; each time would be different.

There was a glow of accomplishment and achievement that Garcia had not felt since those few short weeks he had spent playing in the Row Jimmy after Stella Blue's death. Garcia had forgotten this feeling in the intervening years. He hoped he would never forget it again. There were a peace and a satisfaction he had not known possible. It was obvious that Jorme was feeling something similar, as was the girl. Justin seemed to be less touched by the moment.

The crowd was beginning to disperse; their audience was moving away. Garcia began to play softly at the old guitar, Jorme and Justin joined him, and the music began to build in intensity again . . .

. . . and the night erupted in light. Outside the dingy bar an intense white actinic light flared and grew, seeming to die in intensity as their eyes became accustomed to it, but still bright.

"What the . . . ?" Justin's voice was drowned out in cries of "*Svana! Svana!*"

Svana! Garcia had heard the word during his short stay in the *barraque* five years earlier, but he had never actually seen one of the spontaneous impromptu religious festivals. No one was interested in their music now. A *svana* parade was happening, and that took precedence over anything else in the *barraque*.

He laid his instrument down on the old stand and moved toward the door, following the crowd . . . he who prided himself on never following the crowd.

"You ever seen one of these things before?" he asked
Jorme.

"A couple."

"What is it?" Justin asked.

"*Svana*. It's some kind of religious festival."

"The celebration of rebirth," Jorme said. "The celebration of the day when all men shall be judged and the
barraquistes will receive their true reward."

"Sounds like wish fulfillment to me," Justin said.

"Of course." Garcia smiled. "There's all that religions
ever are."

Jorme looked at him with a hard light in his eyes. "Don't
let any of the *barraquistes* hear you say that. A lot of them
take *svana* very seriously, and they don't take kindly to criticism."

Standing on a chair outside the doorway, Garcia could
see the procession coming down the street. Platforms
carried on the backs of *barraque* men, themselves hidden
by black felt or satin that brushed the dirty bricks of the
street. The platforms covered with flowers and blooms, red
a favorite color, red, the color of blood. In the middle of
the platforms, statues of a man—always the same man, in
different poses, long hair flowing down to his waist—sometimes blond hair, sometimes black, one a rust color, one a
gray. The man was naked to the waist, his face a study of
agony and compassion; he seemed to be grieving for the
pain of the *barraque*—the stone eyes of the statues appeared to sweep through the crowd, always focusing on the
observer, following him, staring at him, judging him, until
the eyes were obscured from sight, and it was time to face
the next statue.

On some floats the statue stood tall, its hand held out in a greeting or blessing. Still the eyes touched Garcia and continued to hold him in that compassionate yet stern gaze. On others the man was sitting with legs crossed, his head crowned with a tiara of thorns from which red roses bloomed like bursts of blood. On one, he rose on one knee, imploring.

Not all the statues were statues, however. Garcia realized that some of them were actual models, holding one pose for hours until muscles had to scream for release and then went beyond that phase to acceptance, the same acceptance of suffering that appeared in their eyes.

On either side of the street, men followed the floats, holding aloft heavy poles that carried the actinic floodlights that had first alerted the *barraquistes* of the *svana* parade's approach. The scent of incense was heavy in the air, so heavy it seemed one could not continue to breathe any longer, the air as thick as purée.

Garcia became aware of others pacing slowly alongside the floats, men and women in soft black hoods, black silk tunics, and woven belts. They were all barefoot; some carried the large candles from which came the incense that clung in the air.

A voice at Garcia's side cut through the incense-laden air. The girl who had been singing with them now was singing to the *svana* floats, to the martyred man whose statues now gazed down at her with compassion and understanding. Another voice, good but not as pure as hers, answered from the other side of the street, and soon the *barraque* night was filled with wordless songs of aching need and desire.

Men stood in the street with tears streaming down their faces, the hard faces of *barraque* men, hard-muscled, intense weary eyes, many of them with their heads covered with handkerchiefs. Their heads were bowed, their bodies bent.

Garcia was aware not only of the girl who stood nearby, her voice once again silent, but also of Augie standing there, his slow mind moved by the spectacle which he had undoubtedly witnessed countless times and yet did not fully understand.

Then the last of the floats was gone and their eyes had to become reaccustomed to the sudden darkness as the sounds and the music receded in the distance.

"That's impressive," Garcia said. "I'd never really felt the power of superstition before."

"It's more than . . ." Jorme was interrupted as someone grabbed Garcia from behind and whirled him around so rapidly that he stumbled as he tried to maintain his balance.

He found himself face to face with a hawk-nosed, lean-faced *barraquiste*, his eyes hard with anger under the kerchief. "What you say?"

"I only . . . I'm sorry . . ."

"The *svana* be more than superstition."

"I didn't mean . . ."

"I hear you play." The *barraquiste* gestured toward the empty bandstand. "You be good, but that give you no right . . ."

"I didn't mean . . ."

A hand slammed against his face. "You listen me, you!

Just 'cause you play so good, you no better than me. You no better than the mud on the streets!"

"Now wait a minute!" Jorme moved his lean body between them, and another *barraquiste* tried to pull him away, but the young autarist shoved him clumsily. The *barraquiste* fell against the brick building, his head making a sickening crunch against the stone. For a moment there was a sphere of silence around them, then there was a grunt of inarticulate rage from the *barraquistes* and Jorme disappeared under a mass of bodies.

Augie began pulling the men away. There was the sound of sirens and the *barraquistes* melted into the night, taking with them the body of their comrade.

Garcia knelt beside Jorme, all the joy and happiness of the evening gone. Blood welled out from a dozen cuts, but the worst seemed to be two stomach wounds. "Garcia? Tell Pentland . . . tell her . . ."

"Yes?"

"I loved her. I really did."

"You'll be all right, Jorme. Damn it. You've got to be all right. Hold on; the police are on their way."

"I've called an ambulance," the owner of the bar said from the entrance.

"You hear that, Jorme? Just hold on."

But Jorme just arched his body in a spasm that had to be painful beyond bearing and let out a groan that expressed far less than the pain he had to be experiencing.

CHAPTER 27

"It looks like we're going to have a busy night," the attendant said as the ambulance flew toward the hospital.

"How's that?" Justin asked as Garcia stared glumly at Jorme's still form. The attendants already had him connected to machines, but the signs were bad.

"The *'quistes* are rioting again. We always have some rough-and-tumbles whenever they have one of these festivals. But it looks like it's going to be worse tonight." Neither Justin nor Garcia said anything, but he continued anyway. "Someone said something about immortality."

"Immortality?" Garcia looked up sharply at the attendant.

"Yeah. Can you beat that? They're saying they want to be immortal and they're going to tear the city down until they are. You ever heard anything so crazy? If that's what religion does to you, I don't want none of it."

Garcia looked back at Jorme. "Is he all right? I thought I saw a needle waver."

"Maybe. These instruments are pretty sensitive. Can't really tell nothing till we get him back to the hospital. I think he'll pull through. Those wounds look pretty superficial. Probably not deep enough to do any real damage."

Garcia didn't know whether or not to believe the attendant. He spoke the words like a well-memorized litany, without any depth or feeling, as though he'd said them to hundreds of people on hundreds of similar occasions.

When they reached the hospital Jorme was whisked away, still unconscious, while Justin and Garcia were led to an office, where a clerk took down details and information. When they were done, forms spit out from the machine at his desk. Justin and Garcia scanned them quickly and put their prints at the bottom.

"How is Jorme?" Garcia asked impatiently.

"Just a minute." The clerk was silent, communing with the hospital's computer. "He is fine. He is resting well."

"He'll recover?"

"We will contact you as soon as there is a change in his condition." Garcia slumped back against the wall, dissatisfied with the clerk's answer, but knowing it would be futile to try to get more out of him. Had Bwire felt this way when Garcia had disappeared into the *barraque*, worrying over the fate of his protégé, damning himself for the part he had played in bringing it about?

The door to the office opened and a policeman walked in. "Mr. Garcia? Mr. Mead? I'm here to escort you home."

"I'm staying here," Garcia said, "until I know what happens to Jorme."

"I don't think that would be wise, sir. There's a riot in the *barraque* and it may well threaten the rest of the city. The hospital will be quite busy and you'll only be in the way." Garcia recognized the tone: they didn't want him here and he would be removed, by force if necessary.

"We will let you know if there is any improvement," the clerk said as they left.

The streets of the city were empty and deserted; only an occasional police car passed them, going in the opposite direction. Once Garcia thought he saw a tank moving on a parallel street but it was too brief a glimpse to be sure.

"It wasn't your fault, Garcia," Justin said when they reached his apartment building. "There was nothing you could've done."

"Sure, Justin."

"I'd come up with you, but I have to get home to my wife. I hate the thought of you being alone up there right now. Why don't you come home with me tonight?"

"No, thanks. I've got to talk to Pentland."

"You could call her from my place."

"Thanks, Justin, but I'd rather be here."

As he rode the elevator to his apartment, he thought about it: *No, it wasn't his fault. Not his fault at all. Who had suggested that they go out for a night on the town? Who had begun the fight by slighting the barraquistes' religion?* No matter what Justin said or thought, Garcia had to take the responsibility. His actions had led inexorably to Jorme's injuries and possible death. He was responsible; he could not ignore it or refuse it.

The thought of calling Pentland and telling her what had happened left a cold lump in Garcia's stomach. He dreaded the call, but it had to be made, and he was the one who had to make it.

As soon as he entered the apartment, however, the supervisor notified him that Shaara had been trying all evening to get in touch with him. "Shall I place a return call?" it asked.

"Not yet. Get me in touch with Pentland LaCroix first."

He sank down wearily in one of the apartment's more comfortable chairs, its form adjusting itself to his body. "Get me a drink." The supervisor began preparing a green joe.

"Garcia?" Pentland's form materialized on the holostage. "Is Jorme there? I've been trying all night . . ."

"He's in the hospital, Pentland."

"No! What happened?"

Briefly, Garcia told her what had happened, making no attempt to play down his own role in his protégé's injuries. She seemed to stiffen as he talked to her about it.

"You don't know . . . ?"

"They said they'd let me know if there was any change."

"I'm going down there."

"Good luck. They kicked *me* out. Let me know as soon as there's any change, will you?"

Pentland paused a moment, her eyes hard and cold. "All right. I will. Goodbye, Garcia."

"Good luck. I hope everything turns out."

He took a long drink from his green joe as Pentland's form faded away. "Do you wish me to contact Shaara now?" his supervisor asked.

"No. Not yet." His head was spinning, still trying to digest the night's events. It seemed no matter what he did, it was wrong. It had been his own desire for excitement and companionship that had driven him out into the night, taking Jorme and Justin with him, willy-nilly, down to the *barraque*. Did he have some kind of death wish? He should have known better. Shaara would never have done anything so silly. But hadn't Shaara's own life become a kind of death in itself?

He looked around the room, where he had once been the court balladeer, the minstrel, where now it seemed he had played the fool instead. He felt like a worm climbing up a rose plant, trying to get past the thorns to the beautiful . . . and edible . . . bloom above. And when he reached one flower, it faded in his grasp and he saw one further up still more beautiful. But to get it he had to struggle through the thorns, the threatened impalement. But without the thorns, there would be no rose, and the worm would wither and die.

"Shaara would like to talk to you."

"What?" Startled by the supervisor's voice, he gripped the glass he had been holding even harder and it shattered, stabbing a painful thorn of plastic into his wrist.

"I have Shaara . . ."

"I know, I know. Let me talk to her."

Shaara materialized on the holostage, facing the chair where Garcia normally sat, but he was behind her, by the bookcase and its emergency exit, nursing the minor wound to his wrist.

"Garcia?" She turned around, looking for him. "Oh, there you are. Where have you . . . ? Darling, have you hurt yourself?"

"Just a little." The blood was a bright red, the vibrant color of life.

"Are you sure?" She peered at him.

"I'm sure."

Her look of concern almost became one of scorn. "I don't know what to do about you. Sometimes you act just like a child."

"Is that what you wanted to talk to me about?"

"No, of course not. I've been trying to get you all night. Where have you *been?*"

"I know. I . . ."

"There's riots going on. They say they're going to be worse than the food riots. There are people outside my father's estate right now."

"Shaara, listen . . ."

"We're all going out to Father's country estate where we'll be safe. I'll have Father send a police flyer over to pick you up and you can join us there."

"Shaara, I'm not going."

"I've been so worried about you, Garcia. How could you do something like this at such a time?"

"Shaara, I'm not going."

"Don't be silly, Garcia. It's not safe here. Of course, this will delay your final operation a bit, but at least you'll be safe."

"I'm not taking the operation, Shaara."

"What do you mean? Of course you are."

Garcia told her what had happened that night, and her terrified face grew even more frightened.

"What's the matter with you, darling? You could have been killed."

"What about poor Jorme? He may die yet."

"Of course. But it's you I worry about. This only makes it clearer: you've got to come out and join us, stay with me permanently. Now. Surely you can see that."

"I can see that I'm not going to take that final operation. I'm going to stay here with Jorme and Justin and Pentland and the people I belong with."

"You belong with me, darling. Don't you want to be immortal?"

"Yes, of course. But . . ." How could he explain it to her? How could he make her understand? She didn't see the life she was living as a kind of death, but to him . . . "Don't you see, Shaara? Without the worm, there would be no rose."

"What are you *talking* about?"

"Never mind. I'm staying here, Shaara. I'm not going to take your damned operation."

"You know what this means, don't you, Garcia? I can't marry you, not if you're not one of us."

"I understand."

"But I love you, Garcia. I really do. I'll always remember you."

"I love you too, Shaara. But I can't live your way."

"Goodbye, my love."

They stood there, each facing the other's intangible image for a long moment, then Shaara broke the connection.

I'll always remember you. He wondered if she really would. Always would probably be a very long time for Shaara.

He began pacing the apartment, but nothing held his at-

tention for very long. He went into the workroom and
stared out at the city for a long moment. There seemed to
be no difference. The riot that was so big could not yet be
seen on this panorama. He took out the old autar and the
old guitar and played each of them briefly, but he could
not finish even one melody.

Something in him called out for action, to do something
more than just play an instrument. He recalled that moment of exaltation back in the *barraque* bar, when the restlessness that had dogged him for so many months was silent and pacified. Now it was back, stronger than ever. He
realized that it would always come back, leaving whenever
he started something new, returning when it was time to
move onward. Only if he were immortal would it be gone
forever.

He returned to the main room, with its false bookcases
and its false fireplace. He remembered when Jorme had
first come to him, with his awkward hands and his nervous
manner. He remembered the strength and beauty of
Jorme's concerts, and he remembered the night that he and
Pentland had stood on the edge of the roof while Garcia
had cowered near the elevator housing.

Bwire's last message to Garcia was on a table next to the
fireplace: *There is something growing inside you, a restlessness. I don't know its exact cause, but please don't disregard it. Follow it, Garcia. It may be hard at times, but
you will not regret it. Reach, strive. Go over the edge.*

Garcia opened the emergency exit and started up the
barren stairway to the roof. Once again he stood in the
doorway of the housing, his heart pounding, looking out

into the windy night. Now, with the panorama of the entire city spread out on all sides, he could see groups of lights he hadn't noticed from his apartment. Down by the river, a glow flickered, and further on there was another fire.

He walked out from the elevator housing, trembling, and the wind hit him full force, threatening to tear him away from the roof into the night. It carried with it the faint smell of smoke, of burning timbers. It paused, as if to gather strength, and in the silence Garcia could hear the sound of sirens and of distant amplified voices, the faint echo of shouts of rage, of tiny cheers.

He looked down over the dizzying edge of the building, where a flimsy rail was all that prevented him from a stomach-wrenching plunge down countless stories. If his heart was pounding now, it was not in fear but in exultation. He was *alive*, come what may, come death and extinction, as surely it must. You can't go back, he thought, and you can't stand still. He had to go forward, or he would surely die. That was where his strength and his art lay, in the constant fight against Death, spitting in its very face, not in conquering it and then living in a fearful immortality. So he would die. So what? In the meantime, he would live life to its fullest, not cringing before every tiny germ.

He started back from the edge of the roof, his mind aglow like the fires in the *barraque*. Bwire's unfinished compositions waited for him, but the melody of another composition was forming in his mind. It would start out in a sad, plaintive key—D minor perhaps—but it would end in a triumphant, surging G major. It would be for autar, guitar, and flute, and there would be a part in it for the beautiful soaring voice of a girl with a scarred face.

He stopped in the doorway of the elevator housing and looked back at the city, watching the flickering glow of the fires and smelling their smoke in the wind.

He would call his composition simply *The Edge*.

Shaara would never understand.